Garr

Also by James Purdy

Novels

63: Dream Palace
Malcolm
The Nephew
Cabot Wright Begins
Eustace Chisholm and the Works
Jeremy's Version
I Am Elijah Thrush
The House of the Solitary Maggot
In a Shallow Grave
Narrow Rooms
Mourners Below
On Glory's Course
In the Hollow of His Hand

Poetry

An Oyster Is a Wealthy Beast
The Running Sun
Sunshine Is an Only Child
Lessons and Complaints

Stories and Plays

Color of Darkness
Children Is All
A Day after the Fair
Proud Flesh
The Candles of Your Eyes

— James Purdy —

GARMENTS THE LIVING WEAR

City Lights Books
San Francisco

GARMENTS THE LIVING WEAR

Copyright © 1989 by James Purdy
All rights reserved

First published by City Lights Books in 1989
Second printing 1990

Cover art: Rainer Fetting's "Kuss II (Kiss II)"
Courtesy of Rainer Fetting

Design by Patricia Fujii

Parts of this book appeared originally in *Christopher Street* and *Art:Mag*.

Library of Congress Cataloging-in-Publication Data

Purdy, James.
  Garments the living wear / by James Purdy.
    p.   cm.
  ISBN 0-87286-240-2 : $16.95. -- ISBN 0-87286-239-9 (pbk.) : $6.95
  I. Title.
  PS3531.U426G37   1989
  813'.54--dc20
                                          89-15782
                                            CIP

City Lights Books are available to bookstores through our primary distributor: Subterranean Company, P.O. Box 10233, Eugene, OR 97440. (503) 343-6324. Our books are also available through library jobbers and regional distributors. For personal orders and catalogs, please write to City Lights Books, 261 Columbus Avenue, San Francisco, CA 94133.

CITY LIGHTS BOOKS are edited by Lawrence Ferlinghetti and Nancy J. Peters and published at the City Lights Bookstore, 261 Columbus Avenue, San Francisco, CA 94133.

For
Jan Erik Bouman
and
Timothy Wilson

Part One

Lloraré
    llorará
        lloraremos!

– popular Cuban song

1

It was the Saracen! Even when he dropped us, he was with us. Even under the thick earth of Santiago de Cuba, he ruled. Our theater flourished only because he showed us what we could be.

Thus Jared Wakeman, the Thespian.

Jared called Mr. Hennings the Saracen by reason of the latter's swarthy complexion. If exposed, for instance, to the midsummer sun, his skin turned black as the darkest African. There was of course the rumor Mr. Hennings was far back on his grandmother's side of Yemeni extraction. But his closer roots were Chicago, Illinois, at least before he became an international financier.

When he darkened my door, Jared Wakeman went on, my life began in earnest. Thinking back on it all, the Thespian almost smiled so that he looked like a pumpkin being carved. Yes, Jared half-bowed, I don't know which of the two was more my fate, Mr. Hennings himself or his wife Estrellita. When Jared got out the name Estrellita, he emitted his hyena-like laugh.

At the time of this story Jared Wakeman was about twenty-six years old, with a mop of corn-colored untrimmed hair and flashy robin's-egg-blue eyes whose intensity made the most self-possessed person look away.

Well, Jared went on, telling how when the economic

barometer was falling all over the world and he himself was hardly more than a street derelict, presto! at that low ebb of fortune he became the owner of a theater in lower Manhattan.

Talk about Maecenases, the Thespian went on with his story, for remember before I became a theater-owner we put on our plays in the very sewers and rat-holes of Manhattan and Brooklyn, and even then the expense cost us an eye and a limb, for a bare-assed derelict on the street consumes thousands of dollars yearly in grub and hand-me-downs.

In Jared's story there were two cataclysmic events, his unexpected inheritance of a theater near Walker Street, Manhattan, and after that windfall, the chilling news that the donor of the house, Edward Hennings, had died hardly before the deed was dry of ink, in Santiago de Cuba. Yet the theater, which Jared thought he desired more than life itself, was, when it was bestowed on him by teams of lawyers, meaningless without the presence and inspiration of the benefactor. It was a mere shell of a mausoleum without resonance or light.

But to go back to Jared's unanswered question, why did this international manipulator of the stock-market (as some claimed him to be), or as more cynical parties dubbed him, this swindler and confidence-man take notice of an unknown Thespian. Not merely take notice of but kowtow to, and kiss the hands of! (Yet coming from so far away at the time of his seeking out Jared, from Europe, the Middle East, he had the honest innocence to affirm he had never heard of the Plague which was decimating the numbers of us Thespians.)

Why, Jared explained, in view of Mr. Hennings total ignorance, at their first meeting, look here, as if the theater didn't have enough problems, Mr. Hennings, almost every other matinee we lose someone to the Pest. There goes our leading man, for instance, dead of it. Or our ingenue – how did we know she used the needle – we found her stiff as a poker by her dressing table, one eye closed, the other accusatory and fulminating horror.

No, Mr. Hennings, aged over ninety-four, and fresh from

his marriage with Estrellita, in Santiago de Cuba, came to *me*. He said, I will back you, look after you, Mr. Wakeman. Don't think I won't.

You would do that? Jared replied in a whisper so faint it would not carry even to the footlights.

I had been waiting for a patron for ten years, Jared often told of his change of fortune. Ten years. Since I was sixteen when I had fallen under the spell of an unknown playwright who wrote his unproduceable plays for me and me alone.

I would have still been all right had it not been for Estrellita, Jared proceeded. I looked into her eyes – laugh at me, go ahead. I looked into her pupils and I was out, a goner. Her eyes were a kind of drab orange-peel color flecked with little brown motes, and her eyelashes seemed to fall to her nostrils. Her mouth looked like some Cuban fruit that has no name in English. Her breath was many flowers, but principally lily of the valley (which later I found out is a rank poison).

My wife, I heard Mr. Hennings's voice. He saw me shudder as he stared at me through his monocle. I recalled then that the bridegroom would never see ninety again, and I took in in one swoop his Saracen complexion, his hunter's eyes (one half-blind), his black but strong teeth.

We don't call her Estrellita too often in Santiago, Mr. Hennings reflected. We call her Lita. But *do* you call her Estrellita if you like, Jared Wakeman.

Then Estrellita spoke, and Jared closed his eyes. He felt a bird was calling. He took her then to his heart like a serum administered by an unknown surgeon.

And then, Jared explains, I took my problem to my heart-throb counseller, Mrs. Sawbridge, in her thirty-room flat, near Gramercy Park. She saw the change in me before I so much as opened my mouth. "You're head over heels," she pronounced her diagnosis.

Peg Sawbridge invited Mr. and Mrs. Hennings to tea, but Edward was tied up in business. Only Estrellita therefore appeared. Jared studied the face of his benefactor, Peg Sawbridge, as the two ladies exchanged handshakes, and he saw the tell-tale signs on the hostess's countenance. Peg was hit hard on looking into those orange-peel Cuban eyes, just as Jared had been.

There is no one like her, Peg Sawbridge admitted after our guest had gone out from us.

Jared and Mrs. Sawbridge embraced with strong, silent feeling. After all at that time, they had a desperate need of one another, Jared urging Peg on with her theatrical ambitions, and she keeping him by her generous emoluments from falling through the cracks and crevices of Manhattan to dereliction and death on the streets.

2

"Mrs. Sawbridge! Mrs. Sawbridge! I do declare!"

Cleo, the eldest of Peg's five daughters, was admonishing her mother as usual. Cleo was Mrs. Sawbridge's most inveterate critic and scold. Unlike her blond mother, Cleo had raven black hair and even blacker pupils surrounded by enormous whites.

"Tell me, mother, where on earth did you come to know *him*! And that dreadful girl! You say she's his *wife*?"

Cleo Sawbridge referred of course to Mr. Hennings and Estrellita.

"Let me change chairs, precious, where the light doesn't shine so in my eyes," Cleo's mother made this excuse, hoping to gain by her interruption some little postponement of Cleo's diatribe. In the sudden silence that followed, Peg smoothed the folds of her soft white dimity dress, and her diamonds sparkled against the snowy fabric.

"Mr. Hennings, my dear child, has been my friend from oh so far back I daren't count the time. Back to Chicago, my dear."

Cleo's lip curled at the mention of Chicago more snottily than had her mother mentioned Timbuctoo. "But to hear Jared talk, Mr. Hennings is *his* friend!" Cleo somehow implied by this statement that her mother must be mistaken, and that Mr. Hennings existed only as Jared's friend.

"No, no, child," Mrs. Sawbridge controlled now her own notoriously bad temper. "Mr. Hennings has only very recently come to take Jared to his bosom. And without my having had any to-do in any of it. That's the beauty of it all. Mr. Hennings found Jared on his own. He's always been partial to theater folk, dear Edward Hennings has."

"You mean mountebanks, don't you, mother, dear."

Peg frowned her deepest scowl, and Cleo smelled danger. "Very well, mother dear, I will take your word for it and call Jared a Thespian in good standing, at least with you."

"Mr. Hennings only rewards genius, Cleo, and I advise you to remember that. You are too young, too sheltered to recognize genius when it appears. Mr. Hennings on the other hand is like a herald angel, ushering in great talent where before the blind world saw nothing and nobody at all."

Corrected, and warned by Peg's growing anger, Cleo shifted to: "But the girl, mother. Estrellita I believe you call her."

"Mr. Hennings calls her by that name, which is, as you say, Estrellita."

"Despite her beauty, mother, she has more than the beginning of a mustache, I observed."

Mrs. Sawbridge was fearfully silent.

"And a vigorous Adam's apple for a young woman."

"Ah yes, and younger than you by several good years," Peg spoke almost too sotto voce to be heard.

"However Estrellita's age and beauty are appraised, mother, Mr. Hennings is far too old to be married, wouldn't you say?"

But Mrs. Sawbridge scarcely was paying any attention to her daughter's bilious harangue. Peg spoke almost as if alone and in soliloquy: "It's as clear as day that Jared has fallen in love with Estrellita." She might have added, "And I am head over heels with Jared".

"I think I could tell you why, mother, Jared loves her if you promise not to chop my head off if I do so."

Mrs. Sawbridge flinched, even paled, but nodded her permission.

"Because, dearest, Estrellita looks so much like a young man!"

All the flesh under Peg Sawbridge's dimity gown moved convulsively. Jared's predilection for young boys was as well-known to her unfortunately as his other weakness for mature women.

"Well, Cleo, if Jared has fallen for Estrellita, I may as well tell you Mr. Hennings is just as smitten with Jared. Just how he is smitten I am at a loss to say. But Edward Hennings talks of nobody now but Jared. He even threatens to buy him a theater!"

The thought perhaps of such largesse caused Cleo to look even more distrait than usual.

"My dearest darling," Peg stared at her daughter and put all the concern she was capable of into her voice, "my precious, eat some breakfast. You look quite in need of nourishment. You must stop this fashionable fasting! Eat something, anything, but stop fasting. You'd be beautiful fat."

"Mother, listen. We must get to the bottom of this," Cleo said, absorbed in the mystery of Estrellita and her marriage. "Where did you say Mr. Hennings found her, and when?"

"In Cuba, dear heart. They were married in Cuba. They say he – Fidel – was at the nuptials."

Cleo was silent, perhaps pretending she had not heard what guest attended the wedding ceremony and then shot out, "Why, Mr. Hennings must be a hundred".

"Whatever you do or say, Cleo, please listen to Mother. Don't tell Jared I have told you he is smitten with Estrellita, or that Mr. Hennings is soft on him.... Remember, sweet, we need all of them! More than you know. Mother's not in good financial condition, I'm afraid. Mr. Hennings has come in the nick of time, and don't you see if he is crazy about Jared and Jared is crazy about his spouse, together all of us will come out in perfectly splendid condition."

17

"I'm quite aware, mother dear, you can't do without Jared. I resigned myself on the score of your affection for him ages ago." As she said this, Cleo choked back the tears of jealousy caused by the pain of knowing her mother cared so much more for the Thespian than for her.

"Don't be like your dead father, Cleo, and stab me to the heart. You know you are my all and everything." She flung open her arms for Cleo to come to her, but her daughter remained cold and still in her big chair.

"Mother needs money," Mrs. Sawbridge spoke anguishedly. "I've never told you on what hideously shaky foundations I rest." She swept her hand in the direction of the vast sumptuousness of her flat. "Cleo, concentrate. If gold were to fall from all the rafters of our home here for days on end without stopping, it would not quite pay off all mother's debts. That's why we need Mr. Hennings and likewise need Estrellita, and finally Jared who is thick with them and yes let me say it thick with me. I am not the mistress of my own life, dear child." And Peg Sawbridge burst into a piteous cacophony of grief, and used her ample sleeve to wipe away her tears.

Calming down a bit and accepting a huge silk handkerchief from Cleo, Peg dried her face.

"So Mr. Hennings has all the money any mortal could want," Cleo attempted to summarize and close the subject. But her mother began again:

"Ah, yes, think of it all, love. He's a citizen of the world. The financial world, at least, Zurich, London, Baghdad, are the least of it. He has homes in ten countries, in each of which he's as well known as the face of the ruling sovereign. And of late, why don't ask me, he comes and goes in Cuba as if he owned the island. He says the climate is perfect for his blood pressure and arthritis. Pish! I sometimes wonder what is under his monocle. I mean perhaps it's wires to the world's treasury." For no accountable reason Mrs. Sawbridge again began sniffling and daubing her eyes.

"Mother, please! Let's not sob and cry. I beg you."

Swallowing her tears Peg spoke in her most imploring tone: "Whatever you do, Cleo, and remember your own security and well-being are at stake here – do *not* say anything to any of them, Edward, Jared, or Estrellita about our talk today. It will sour things!"

"Sour things?" Cleo shouted as if she had been accused of a crime.

"Don't for God's sake say, for instance, to Jared that you think Estrellita looks like a boy. And don't say to Edward that Jared is only a mountebank or that I am head over heels with Jared! For once, my angel, be circumspect. Don't touch on any of these subjects for your topics of conversations! Spare all of us! Be good. Or, and listen well...."

Cleo rose now and made toward the door. "I know, mother, if I don't behave you will disinherit me!' She turned, however, before going out the door and shot a look of rage and reproach at her mother.

"I will talk to them only of the weather, rest assured," Cleo sneered, "the clouds and the moon and the fixed stars." Then the door crash-slammed behind Peg's daughter.

19

3

"I was about to write you a letter," Mrs. Sawbridge spoke in a voice loud enough to reach four storeys down to the street.

Peg addressed Jared Wakeman, who stood in the threshold of her front parlor.

"Not one of *those* letters, for Pete's sake," he registered a kind of genuine horror. "Your letters are worse than Cleo's scoldings. And they are a permanent record besides. So don't write letters! Scold me viciously like Cleo scolds you, but keep your pen dry, Peg."

He kissed her now rather thoroughly across her mouth and cheeks.

"But I can never remember all the things I have to accuse you of at a face-to-face meeting," Peg went on half jocularly. "A letter gets it all out of me. Besides you can always tear up a letter, and it becomes as insubstantial as Cleo's scolding."

Jared sat down, removed his wide-brimmed hat, and held it carefully in his right hand as if he were holding it for perhaps Mr. Hennings. He saw Peg's swift look of admiration of the hat and especially its blue-gold ribbon. "You'd like to wear it," he said and flung it at her. She grinned and put it on and sort of purred.

"Now see here, Jared. You cannot be interested in this person. Everyone's gossiping that you are. Put it like this, sweetie, I am responsible not just for your career, I am responsible for you being happy."

"Happy?" he roared, got up and seized his hat from off her head, and slammed it on, almost over his ears. "Happy," he muttered between his teeth. "St. Peter and all the saints could never see that achieved. And the *person* you refer to is I suppose Estrellita."

"Even if she was not somebody else's wife, Jared," Peg was incapable of stopping herself now. "Even if...."

"I'm not in love with anybody."

"You are! You are! Don't I know you, Jared. From deep down. And after all we've been through together. I don't want to see you hurt."

"What hypocrisy! What rot! Can't I admire beautiful people without you claiming me for yourself all the time."

"All right! Love her, run off with her, ruin yourself. Remember only *he* can help us at this stage of the game. Just look around you! Everything you see is mortgaged to the rafters. I'm through, I tell you. But if we keep Edward I may at least have a roof over my head. Listen here, he owns the half of the Caribbean. We need patrons, Jared!" She screamed now because he had risen and walked toward the door. "Don't you dare to leave me when I am explaining business.... We need patrons, I repeat, and you've said it too a thousand times. And we need him. And we have him, if you'll believe, angel!"

"Good enough! All right, I say all right." He began to finger his cigarette. He had sworn off smoking at least ten times in the past five years, and always came back to the habit. He would hold an unlighted cigarette often, hoping it would keep him from finally striking up and smoking.

"See," he mocked her. "My knees are practicing to bend before you!" Here he half-knelt, and while in this position he continued: "I want to put on plays more than anything in the world I suppose. You know it."

"Suppose, my eye," she chided. "You *know*. That's why I love you, Jared. You're so possessed! So total."

She rose now and came to where he was actually in a full

21

kneeling posture. She kissed him on the forehead, and then on both his cheeks. "Be a good boy. Don't love *her*. Love anybody but her."

"Well, Peg, is that all for today" he wondered and rising, turned away and stared at his hat suspiciously, even pulling roughly on its handsome ribbon.

"I am so afraid of her, Jared. If she is a *her*, that is."

He wheeled about, his face flushing.

"What are you talking about now, Peg?"

"Never you mind." And Mrs. Sawbridge checked herself.

Jared came over and pulled her toward him roughly.

"What did you mean, Peg." He was almost hysterical.

Just then the phone rang, and she gave him a silent adieu with two fingers pressed against her lips on which she had neglected as yet to put French lip rouge.

"I guess softening of the brain must explain it all, Peg," Jared spoke to her retreating figure, and he strode to the door, opened it and went out, leaving behind his hat and not bothering to close the door.

4

"So you are blessed, dear Edward, with a young wife," Mrs. Sawbridge addressed Mr. Hennings as they began their first "serious" meeting together. She had chosen the seldom-used very intimate small sitting-room at the far rear of her many rooms.

Mr. Hennings kept on his enormous Panama hat, with Peg's permission, for the wide brim he told her would protect his delicate vision from the New York glare.

When there was no response from Edward to her first comment, Peg found herself going on with: "She looks at you as if you were her only refuge – Estrellita I mean."

"Perhaps." He was very distant. "But safe harbor means everything to a girl like Estrellita, Peg."

"But you're more than safe harbor for her, unless I miss my guess."

"Well, then, let me tell you." He chose his next words bending his head under his hat's brim which looked big as an awning. "Estrellita Fuentes y Fonseca," he said after clearing his throat noisily, "that girl has lived through more history than many a head of state. She has known warfare in the hills and on the sea, pillage, prison, indignity, indecency, famine – and through it all she has kept her own character."

As Mr. Hennings rattled on, Mrs. Sawbridge studied his Saracen (to use Jared Wakeman's phraseology) features.

Swarthy! Was ever a man so swarthy? Yet she was not afraid of him or squeamish about being so close to him. Had he worn a turban he would have been all of Arabia Felix for her, she thought. Yet his family has been in the coal business in Chicago for generations!

"You fuss, Peg," Mr. Hennings lifted the brim of his hat and then pushed it even more tightly downward, "you worry and fume that people will fall in love with so beautiful a girl, and she'll run off with one of her devotees. But what Estrellita loves is not romance, dear Peg, but safe harbor. That's me."

"Her beauty –" Mrs. Sawbridge began, for she thought it wise to praise Estrellita now, but Edward cut into her speech.

"Ah well, her exquisite coloring and complexion you refer to," Mr. Hennings smiled cooly grateful for Peg's admiration, "that coloring, my dear is Basque. She goes back to countless generations of shepherds and shepherdesses, and one of the things I noted about her immediately when I rescued her from prison was she smells of the fields of Galicia. She is a shepherdess! I often tell her she should always carry a shepherd's crook."

"Ah, well, my dear Edward," Mrs. Sawbridge pretended concern and fear, "I'm afraid New York will not prove to be Galicia or even old Havana."

"Are you still harping on the danger of Estrellita's being taken from me, or are you merely throwing out the well-worn caveat that New York is the greatest criminal and most untidy, if not most filthy metropolis of the civilized world."

"Ah, well, Edward, you may denigrate old Manhattan if you care to. Those are your words, not mine. Yet aren't we glad, my dear friend, that we knew New York when it was in its way truly wonderful?"

"But that was *then*, Peg, and a long-ago *then*. I regard the city today as a tunnel of tar. One can't quite quarrel with a tunnel if that is what it is. One turns on the lamp and waits."

"Oh, but it had something once before all the glass boxes came and anthropoids ruled the streets."

"Let us go to more immediate matters," Mr. Hennings was abrupt. "There is this one person who holds my undivided attention, Peg."

"I knew, my love, you would come to him." Despite her wish to encourage Mr. Hennings her voice almost wailed, then broke.

"Of course I realize he is your protégé, Peg, and I don't want to encroach upon your territory. In the end I yield to you in all things of this kind. You know me.

"But," Mr. Hennings was pitiless, "he must be mine, Jared Wakeman. I put him at the top of my own priorities. You may claim him of course as your own. But I must have him as my find and my genius. And I must promote him, needless to say."

"My dear Edward, excuse me, but may I say *you* sound like the one who is smitten."

The pain of knowing another loved Jared caused Peg to tremble and as she reached in her panic for her palm-straw fan, she dropped it. When Mr. Hennings handed it back to her, she realized either he had not heard her remark or paid it no heed.

"As I say, I want to back him, Peg. I hate the present-day theater, hate all the arts today, indeed as I hate New York, the tar tunnel, but I want to back someone who is the antithesis of the Metropolis, don't you see. And of course a genius. I believe in Jared implicitly and I therefore throw caution to the winds."

Without warning, Mr. Hennings rose and bidding Peg rise also he hugged her tightly to him with the result his monocle fell (attached to a silk ribbon) to his collar, and he kissed her brow gently, murmuring: "We shall have theater, my darling. We shall throw money as well as caution to the winds... you shall star in every production. Yes, Jared has told me of your late awakening to the histrionic art.

"But wonderful Peg," Mr. Hennings spoke more soberly now, and extricated himself from his embrace of Mrs. Sawbridge. "I read your thoughts as easily as a hunter foresees the change in weather.... You fear for me that Jared is smitten with Estrellita ... I want Jared to be smitten with her. There! That lifts a burden from your poor brain! I knew it would. Can't you still see Estrellita can only be mine, sweet. Only mine. Let Jared love her! Nothing will come of it."

"All the same, wonderful friend, I will keep an eye on her, and a close watch that nothing will harm her." Peg spoke with pained altruism.

"Estrellita will elude your chaperoning of her, Peg, but keep all the watch you please, short of locking her up."

Peg went to a small cupboard and brought out a bottle of Vichy Celestine, poured Edward half a glass, and handed it to him. He drank in little sips much like a bird, even throwing his head back like one.

"You forget how far back I remember you, Edward," Mrs. Sawbridge reminded him, drinking direct from the bottle of Vichy. "Up until now you've always had men attendants. Or attendants too young to be men. I remember that colored boy you had from one of the South Carolina islands. He spoke only Gullah. Or so you told me."

"Your memory is phenomenal, Peggy," Edward sighed after smacking his lips loudly from the Vichy Celestine.

"And I recall too that you told me the Gullah-speaking boy was early on drafted into the army, Edward, and that when his headquarters company saw he could speak only Gullah, after weeks of giving him potatoes to peel, the colonel had to release him for the chap didn't know squads right from squads left."

Edward smiled amusedly. "That was Sully," he almost whistled the name. "Yes, Sully the Illustrious I called him. I met him on the streets of Charleston, South Carolina, not too long ago. He had changed very little. From six feet away he still looked like a boy, or as you would say too young to be a man. What are you doing now, Sully? I inquired. I repair merry-go-round horses over there, he told me as he pointed to some once grand now dilapidated mansion. What an out-of-the-way profession you have finally settled for, I applauded his rise in the world. He grinned proudly showing every one of his pearl-white teeth not one of which had ever seen a dentist. But as he talked on about merry-go-round horses and calliopes, I do believe his English had become even less understandable than when he was my valet."

"That is another phenomenon about your staff," Peg Sawbridge pointed out this anomaly. "You always, Edward, are partial to those who can barely speak English or indeed any other language. I have noticed Estrellita is no exception to this rule."

"Wrong, wrong, Peggy. Estrellita knows both English and Spanish and can read menus in French and Italian. But she is shy. Pitifully shy."

"Ah well, what matter. And since you say she is comfortable with Jared, and you are comfortable with him." And having uttered this piece of wisdom, Peg threw up her hands and rolled her eyes.

"But it has also broken my heart, Peg, to see you so infatuated with Mr. Wakeman. That is it broke my heart on first becoming aware of your loving him so dearly. How could she? I said to myself. What future has Peg with a Thespian.... Now I realize my mistake.... You have every future with him."

"You seem to feel, Edward, dear, that everything where I am concerned is amour. But there is more to me than amour, I tell you! See here," she said, and warned him not to interrupt by raising her right hand bearing the four emerald rings, "I was in dry-dock before Jared appeared, and my timbers were turning to powder. Jared saw me as an actress *before* I loved him. The sound of the curtain going up, however tattered and moth-eaten, knocked off thirty years from me and my voice returned to its pristine resonance. Furthermore, our audiences clapped their hands till their fingers were raw against their rings. When I appeared as Aurelia Wilbur in the last-century melodrama, and extricated the hatpin from my ostrich-plumed chapeau, the entire auditorium went mad. I didn't wait for curtain calls. I went to where Jared stood watching me from his part of the wings. I knelt down like the Pontiff in Poland, and kissed and kissed his grimey clodhoppers. He allowed my gesture only to please me! Yes, he didn't say, 'Don't, Peg, don't,' but allowed my embrace of his clogs."

"Ah, well, Peg, I bow to you both!" Mr. Hennings polished his monocle.

"Does Estrellita give you as much as Jared gives me, Edward?"

Mr. Hennings folded his massive but slightly withered arms: "I require retinue, Peg. She is always at her station."

"Why have you changed sexes this time in your choice of servants?" Peg referred to the fact that in the past all his valets had been men.

Edward Hennings gave her a severe, almost maniacal look of reproach, and the look frightened her, or at least discomposed her for a moment.

"To go back to our conversation," he spoke icily, "let me emphasize over again a point. I don't at all mind Jared's attention to Estrellita. It's you who do. Be at peace, Peg, nothing can come of their knowing one another."

"Except he loves her!" she wailed. "Isn't that enough bad news for ten years."

"If you knew all I know, Peg, you'd know all the pages are blank in their book where amour is concerned."

"Blank or full, I cannot bear it," she was more quiet now in her grief.

5

"No, no, not that brat now with all the rest that is going wrong!" Mr. Hennings had cried when the receptionist announced on the telephone that Miss Cleo Sawbridge was in the lobby asking to see him. However, he admitted her.

"You will never know how Mama has changed," Cleo began at once in the pearl-gray of the Manhattan twilight which was descending on Mr. Hennings' ten-room suite overlooking the forest-like vista of Central Park.

"You forget I knew your mother before you were born or even thought of, Cleo. Before even perhaps she married your father. You forget also that your mother was famous as a singer before your father became an internationally known art dealer."

Cleo, usually an iceberg of restraint, daubed her eyes with a cocktail napkin she found on the table before her.

A young man entered bearing a tray of hot chocolate.

"Violate your diet, Cleo." Mr. Hennings was severe when he saw Peg's daughter hesitate to take a cup. "And drink all of it," her host chided.

Cleo sipped at first, then drank a hearty swallow.

"I could forgive Mama's being an actress, I suppose," Cleo began with some of the frothy chocolate on her upper lip. "But don't you see, Mr. Hennings, it's how she became an actress! And you surely must see *him* for what he's worth!"

In her anger she finished the cup of chocolate, and at a signal from Mr. Hennings, the valet poured her another.

"You refer to Jared, of course," Mr. Hennings prompted her like a bored theater director.

"Who else?" Cleo nodded vigorously and in her misery drank another swallow of the chocolate. "There's only Jared now. He's taken Mama over. She looks right past me when I come into the room when he's sitting at her knees. I could be air! *Jared this, Jared that!*"

"Your mother is terribly fearful that Jared loves my wife," Mr. Hennings tested Cleo on this score while they were on the subject of the Thespian.

"He can love nobody but his own self-image and ambition," she was firm on this. She thought for a moment. "Still, since he's a graduate blackguard, you would be perhaps wise to be on your guard, Mr. Hennings. He has a way of making both men and women fall for him! How, don't ask me!"

But Cleo's warning had made if not a direct hit on Edward Hennings, a considerable dent in his armor. He spoke almost to himself then: "Estrellita and I have been through so much. We were in prison together in Havana. Our escape, Cleo, could easily be the subject of films and operas. But she is so close to me beyond what we've endured at the hands of the world's powers. But adultery, unfaithfulness, sin itself are meaningless to both of us. And even were she to fall, she could only eventually fall into my arms again. And what could Jared Wakeman after all give a woman like Estrellita?"

"Perhaps it's the fact he can give her nothing which may betray her," Cleo leaned forward in pronouncing this somewhat dreadful perception.

Mr. Hennings fidgeted now. Cleo saw as she sipped her third cup of chocolate she had got to him on the score of Estrellita and Jared if not on that of Peg Sawbridge's dereliction as a mother.

"Rest assured, Cleo, I will confer with your mother about all of this." He drew an over-large timepiece from his vest pocket and stared at it lengthily. "But you must not deprive your mother of her new career," he warned. He held the timepiece in the palm of his hand a while before putting it back in its place in his vest. "She will act, Cleo, she will live only before the footlights. If you spoil her new calling, she and you will be in great trouble. If you make her renounce acting, she will have nobody then but Jared! Think this over carefully, weigh your course of action! Perhaps you should go away."

"Away? And where, Mr. Hennings! I only love New York. I've been away besides, at scores of finishing schools. I say I've been away enough!"

"You are too close to your mother. You must find your own calling, your own way."

"I must protect her!"

"No, no, that is something you cannot do. Imprison her is what you mean. You must *abdicate*, Cleo, if you love your mother. I'm not sure you do."

"Abdicate, go away! Why not tell me to shoot myself? I don't know how you can be so cold and unfeeling."

She rose.

"Eat one of these bonbons before you depart. Taste it at least."

After a long hesitation she picked up the sweetmeat and put it in her mouth.

"You will thank me one day for talking to you like this," Mr. Hennings assured her as he came laboriously up from his sitting position.

"And you may thank me one day for warning you about the danger Estrellita faces with Jared." Cleo spoke throatily through a mouth full of candy.

Mr. Hennings gave out a vibrant laugh like that of some untalented actor. "Do you know how many persons fall in love with Estrellita? At least two per day. And do you know what their loving her does? It only binds her more tightly to my protection! In fact she fears any closeness but mine."

Cleo's mouth moved with a response, but closing her lips tight, she allowed herself only the following dictum: "All the same, Mr. Hennings, Jared is not anyone either you or she has known before. I at least acknowledge the strength of his powers."

She snatched up another bonbon and was gone.

6

"I don't know why you think this is a *row*," Mrs. Sawbridge spoke with even more indignation than was usual for her. She was addressing Jared Wakeman who stood near the threshold of the front parlor. He was complaining that he had been "summoned" like one of Mr. Hennings' countless valets.

"Summoned after all I've done for you!" He kept repeating this "outrage".

"I acknowledge all you've done for me," Peg raised her voice to its highest pitch. "You never, Jared, admit all that I've done for you. And some think it is considerable."

"I don't know who the *some* are, Peg, but you certainly think what you've done for me is more than considerable. Colossal I believe would be what you call it."

"But, to change the subject," Jared spoke cooly, and undoing the top button of his pongee shirt he sat down on a footstool near his benefactress. "Look, I have finally decided why Estrellita of old Havana is such a necessity to Edward Hennings." He warmed to his discovery: "It all at once hit me like the solution to a Chinese puzzle. Once the puzzle's solved, you can't fathom how you didn't solve it at first try."

"So what is the solution, dear?" Mrs. Sawbridge was now peaceable.

"She holds him to this life as a string holds a kite."

Mrs. Sawbridge nodded, waited.

"It's more than marriage, Peg. They're like Orpheus and Eurydice. Even hell itself won't be able to keep them apart."

Mrs. Sawbridge tightened the ruby earring on her right earlobe.

"For," he went on gleeful, "whichever one of them goes first under earth's crust, the other will be, don't you see, *lost*!"

"Dear Jared, with all the fortune Edward will leave Estrellita, she'll be *lost*?"

"You surprise me, Peg," he began his scolding tone. "She'll be worse than lost. Should Mr. H. die, Estrellita will immediately follow thereafter. They breathe through the same pair of lungs."

Mrs. Sawbridge bowed her head. As in their play rehearsals, in the end he always illuminated her part to her. Now he had illuminated the parts of Estrellita and Edward until she wondered why she hadn't seen the truth of his observation from the beginning.

"Oh, Jared, as usual you are right," Peg grumbled. "The puzzle's solved, and I was in the dark.

"Jared," Mrs. Sawbridge's voice fell almost to a baritone now, "let me say this: *you must not love that girl*! For your own sake!"

Instead of emitting his disgusting kind of laugh he gave out a variety of snort which was even more offensive, if possible, to her. "But what difference would it make to them!" Jared began fixing her with his stare, "how could it reach to Hennings and his Estrellita, if what you say is true. Nothing can part them!"

"But you are always falling in love, Jared, with people who can't give you anything in return. There was Moon Silverspoon, the television star of brief notoriety, and more lately, a California stripper named Brad Sternoff."

Jared toyed with his cowlick. "I can't love you all the while, Peg," he spoke rather lamely for him.

"*All the while*!" She scoffed and laughed now almost as indecorously as he did.

"Mr. Hennings doesn't care a jackstraw who loves Estrellita for the simple reason he's the only man probably since the dawn of time who can be sure of the faithfulness of his spouse. The two of them already belong, you might say, to immortality."

Peg's attention strayed back to the ceaseless litany that occured between her and Cleo. "If only," she could hear Cleo's voice now even above Jared's, "if only you didn't love Jared Wakeman. What would Father say if he knew?" And for a brief interlude Peg thought of her husband. Dead, he had no power over her in this world or in any world to come. Once Mr. Sawbridge had died his only significance to her was the rather indecent amount of his legacy left her in worldly goods. He had collected so much art that Mrs. Sawbridge had once quipped that the lawyers to his estate could easily spend twenty-four hours a day merely going over the receipts of the cash which rained down.

"We are so rich, Cleo, darling," Peg had once remarked, "that with each breath we draw we are buried a little more alive in gain."

7

Peg Sawbridge loved to reminisce also about the time when Jared Wakeman had only a bowing acquaintance with her. She had been for him then grand and distant, if not unapproachable. He lived then on West 46th Street near Eleventh Avenue. Hell's Kitchen at that time was so dangerous that she visited him in an armored car. Her chauffeur carried several firearms. Yet once inside Jared's building under its ruined skylight one felt safe and even in luxurious surroundings. His landlord was reputed a Cherokee Indian from a Georgia chain gang, but when she asked Jared if this was true he gave his thin line of a smile. Jared's poverty was so overwhelming it had for her the epic nature of royal lineage. He clung, she saw at once, to his poverty like misers to hidden gold and rubies.

Then gradually he had become part of her retinue, and from her retinue he graduated to her lover.

"She does not really keep me, bear in mind," Jared constantly emphasized to his own many lovers.

Then the Plague came, and he lost his lovers. They dropped like the leaves from sycamores in November.

Being told of the Plague, Mrs. Sawbridge would stare at her emeralds, or pull on her amber beads, and say: "I am a century behind in all this.... Of course in my day we had dread viruses, called by a mealy-mouthed press 'social diseases.' Syphilis, gonorrhea, and others whose names escape me."

Jared Wakeman's permanent state at that time was he usually did not have enough change in his pocket even to purchase a subway token. He never paid his Cherokee landlord a cent for his rather ample apartment.

"Imagine," Peg would say to him, as they sat in those days under his ruined skylight and his poverty stared out at her. "A dollar you say for a subway?" (She rode only then as now in limousines.) "I can remember when it was a nickel. Overpriced then. But a dollar! Granted a dollar is like a penny was then. Ridiculous. The city should pay its riders to step down into that hole. The last time I went into the underground I knew the city was through, and probably the nation. Any civilization with such an underground has cashed in its last check."

"I keep my eyes closed, Peg, when I go down," Jared mumbled. Although an actor of great talent he hardly ever opened his mouth wide enough for words to escape.

But it was not his extreme poverty which drove him into the arms of Mrs. Sawbridge. It was the Plague, the Pest which was relentlessly carrying off most of his lovers. The Pest made him hers.

Head over heels! people said of Mrs. Sawbridge's love of the impecunious almost unknown Thespian, Jared Wakeman. Madly, hopelessly enamoured at her age!

Beautiful men and women shudder when they realize their thirtieth birthday is a year or so away. But Mr. Hennings sometimes went cold as a gravestone when he thought that in four to five years he would be one hundred. It was about the time of this realization that he felt the need of a hot climate. His Zurich, Switzerland days were after all over. He had made all the money he could make. And the very sight of snow on a mountain made his heart haul to a stop.

So the Caribbean opened up for him – Cuba. And when life in Havana proved too complicated even for an American of his international credentials, he drifted to Key West. It was like a fragment of Havana, inferior of course, ruined like New York by the developers, but with much the same climate, and the heat made him not think of his hundredth birthday. He didn't know how old Estrellita was, nor did she. The Revolution, the following upheaval had made her somewhat unknowledgeable about her family or her exact date of birth, and so the two, almost a century apart, were in flight together.

When in July even Key West was too hot for him, Mr. Hennings always came to Manhattan. The heat was almost as great, the air was foul, and oh the decline! He had remembered New York in his own mind when it had been in flower. Now it was a collection of glass boxes, its government ruled largely by crooks, its citizens picked to the bone by insatiable landlords, the streets surrendered to roving packs of hoodlums and uncollected garbage, derelicts asleep on the walks day and night as in New Delhi, and rising from all this ordure the new Orientals with their vegetable stalls.

Yet despite his loathing of Manhattan, Mr. Hennings came dutifully every year from the Caribbean to put money into the wasted palms of artists and writers, and finally actors like Jared Wakeman, and Mrs. Sawbridge who was young enough to be his daughter. Her beauty and seeming youthfulness pleased him immoderately. To think she was talented also as an actress mystified and delighted him. And with Jared, the two of them, he realized, achieved something queerly grand in histrionics. He would support them, therefore.

Money to burn! This description of him was more irksome to Mr. Hennings than pleasing. He worshipped money, of course. He was known to stoop down in dirty gutters to pick up a penny discarded by a beggar or a schoolboy. But he would never burn money! He knew how hard it had been to amass his own incredible fortune.

And thinking of money burning and money being flung to them for their theatricals, Peg placed her arms around Edward Hennings, whispering: "How, my dearest, could I act for anybody else after all, but him. Don't you see? I can be an actress only under Jared's tutelage and supervision. And when he fails to keep an eye on me when I am on stage the words falter in my mouth, and what I'm doing is not even dumb-show!"

Mr. Hennings could not (he harped on this string) get over the decline of the metropolis of Manhattan. He remembered *her* (he reminded Peg) when she was absolutely dynamic. Peg did not dare cavil, but she felt Manhattan had never been as wonderful as Edward recalled her, or as decayed and paralyzed as he found her today, *she* and *her* being of course the fallen city.

But Edward gag-mouthed Peg's differing with his view. He recalled Dublin in the 1920s, New Delhi at almost any epoch, Barcelona during the bread riots, and Berlin before the Third Reich. Manhattan, he shouted, was more tawdry than any of the forementioned cities at their worst.

Very little caused Mrs. Sawbridge to lose her sang-froid, perhaps nothing, but she became open-mouthed, almost adenoidal when, during Mr. Hennings' lectures on the fall of Manhattan from his standards, she turned her gaze at first only briefly, then to a full stare at Jared Wakeman, who had stolen in almost unobserved during Edward's diatribe. Jared had taken a seat by Estrellita on the settee and was holding her arm so tightly that he finally succeeded in pushing her sequined sleeve above her biceps. Biceps she certainly had and above them was a tattoo of a hummingbird and a network of beautiful but very pronounced blue veins.

Mr. Hennings must have seen, Peg thought, half-blind or not, what Jared was doing, but if so it only catapulted the international financier into another attack on the filth, noise, corruption and tasteless mediocrity of Manhattan. Even when Jared kissed the veins of Estrellita in the crook of her arm Mr. Hennings made no indication of surprise or disapproval. In fact he yawned during Jared's lavish kisses of his wife.

"Ah, well!" Peg managed to get out, and her voice was loud

as a fire bell. Everybody got silent. Jared dropped Estrellita's arm, which fell to the cushions beside her like that of a rag doll.

"But wasn't Manhattan bad during the depression, Edward, dear?" Mrs. Sawbridge ad-libbed now desperately.

"Why, it was positively gay in comparison with now," Edward replied jauntily. "There was energy in the air, and even if young men sold apples on the street, there was a feeling things would get right. People helped one another, there were manners from the lowest classes to the upper. The subways were clean and riders well-dressed and polite. No one as now appeared naked in fashionable hotel lobbies. The theater flourished for we had playwrights then, and the actors did not mumble or scratch their rectums before the footlights. And the popular music of the day – it was glorious and spoke to all, not just to drug-fiends."

"But Edward," Peg interjected, trying not to see Jared kissing Estrellita's knees now. "Nothing can stand still, dear friend. Perfection itself would weary one."

Then, as Peg remarked later, just as in one of their own cut and dried play rehearsals, Edward Hennings gave some imperceptible motion to Estrellita and husband and wife both rose at the same moment, gave affable goodbyes to both Peg and Jared, and were gone.

8

Mrs. Sawbridge's many sorrows appeared to her at times during her long hours of insomnia as twigs which she carried in her mouth like a bird, depositing each day's collection in a huge, nest-like structure which was, she supposed, her mansion and her life.

But in that immense structure of twigs collected from her days of sorrow was a new sorrow. Not only was she tormented by her hopeless love for Jared Wakeman, she bore a new torment, her certain knowledge that Cleo loved Jared as hopelessly – no, more hopelessly than she did. *Mother and daughter both in love with one terrible man*! And that terrible man in turn in love with Estrellita.

Mrs. Sawbridge's discovery of her daughter's secret came about in fact as a result of her insomnia. At three in the morning, still unable to so much as doze off, she had finally risen in order to take a short stroll down one of the interminably long corridors which led to nearly all the bedrooms of her establishment. Holding a tiny Chinese flashlight she was walking past Cleo's bedroom when she heard her daughter's voice. Waiting a few moments, and then hearing nothing more, and alarmed even more by the silence, Peg opened the door. Her daughter lay stark naked on her king-sized bed. At first the thought crossed her mother's mind that Cleo had taken poison, she looked so pale and still, her nipples giving the impression they had been drained of blood.

In her turmoil, Peg almost fell to the bed beside her daughter.

Cleo's eyelids fluttered wildly as she muttered, "Jared, you are my own, my dearest! Take me in your arms again." Then, coming out of her slumber and her dream, Cleo woke to stare into the tiny beam of the Chinese flashlight, and her mother's eyes. And then, so unlike her haughty, independent nature, Cleo threw herself into her mother's arms.

"It's all right, precious," Peg smoothed her daughter's hair and kissed her solemnly on the mouth.

"Tell me I am a fool, mother. Chastise me. That is what I've always needed from you, punishment."

Peg only held her more tightly to her. "I only love you more dearly," Peg released her hold slightly.

"What must we do, mother? What *can* we do?"

"Wait for time, darling. Let time settle everything."

"Time is endless."

"More even than my folly for caring for *him*," Peg moved a little away from Cleo, "is this damnable insomnia."

"Isn't that love's doing also?" Cleo had never been so benign.

"Ramon laughs at my claim of not being able to sleep," Peg spoke in a lighter tone. "He says he sees me taking little naps many times during the long, tedious afternoons here."

Peg was hardly aware that Cleo was now having her first long and thoroughly refreshing crying jag. Her tears wet her nakedness and splashed over to her mother's cerise dressing gown.

They held hands convulsively then, and desperately turned to subjects of consequence to either of them.

"Mr. Hennings says I should go away," Cleo had risen and put on a dressing gown of the same color as her mother's.

"You haven't told him how you feel about Jared?" There was a touch of the old high-and-mighty manner for a moment in Peg's voice.

"God no. I've shared my secret only with Morpheus. But as you know all too well, Mr. Hennings gets to the bottom of everything."

"I don't want you to go away, Cleo, ever. Especially now." Her mother kissed her again and again. "Stay with me while time and fortune work for both of us."

Cleo sat smoking a left-over cigarette.

"I fear I have made another mistake," Peg came now to one of the other subjects which possibly had exacerbated her insomnia. "And I didn't consult you on the matter because I feared you would say no."

"But for heaven's sake, mother, what is it?" Some of Cleo's own old ill-temper had returned.

"You won't be furious with me, sweetheart?" Peg waited until Cleo had finished her half-consumed smoke and found another used one to light.

"I have invited Mr. Hennings and his wife to move in with us. Temporarily at least." She dared not look at her daughter. "I couldn't very well say no after all he's done for us. It seems they've been robbed four times in their hotel on Sixth Avenue. The management practically laughed in their faces when Mr. Hennings told them of the repeated break-ins. You forget this is New York, the manager informed Edward and Estrellita. We can do nothing about crime or break-ins in our suites here.... So, Cleo, at the risk of disobeying you, dear, I have invited them to stay with us. We'll all live through it somehow."

"Of course you'll live to regret it," Cleo said, but Peg was almost overwhelmed by her daughter's lack of resentment and her failure to scold.

"And you'll forgive your poor mother?"

Cleo blew kisses through her cigarette smoke.

Mrs. Sawbridge was astonished at how little the Hennings brought with them. Estrellita carried what was a rather faded although luxurious overnight bag, and Mr. Hennings brought with him only a pair of cowhide valises.

"I suppose everything else is still in Zurich or Havana" Peg muttered under her breath.

The Hennings might as well have been in their Sixth Avenue hotel suite for the rooms Mrs. Sawbridge assigned them to were every bit as posh, large and lavishly furnished.

9

The coming of the Hennings to her mansion only increased Peg Sawbridge's propensity to insomnia. Both Estrellita and Edward made constant demands on her, for one thing, and Estrellita's extreme beauty and strange charm plunged Peg into a melancholy, endless reverie.

One night very late, on her way to her private bathroom, and having forgotten to put on her glasses, Peg mistakenly opened the door leading to the apartments of the Hennings. Confused by her mistake, instead of retreating she made still another blunder of opening the door which led directly to Estrellita's sleeping room. Stretched out amongst cushions and scant draperies was someone, Peg could barely make out who, someone whose extreme loveliness struck her dumb. The effulgence of the sight indeed seemed all at once to have restored Peg's eyesight. Her knees began to give and she felt herself sinking down beside the recumbent figure pressed against the cushions.

The sleeper stirred and with its nervous hand pushed away thin draperies covering the groin.

Peg felt her eyesight must be playing her tricks, for looking down where the draperies had lain she took in an even greater glory than the sleeper's long gold-brown hair and red and gold coloring, a penis and scrotum resembling those of the child-gods of Raphael.

At the same moment of this revelation, Estrellita raised up and took Peg's lips in her own and like a person who has been without water for hours on end drank thirstily from the older woman's mouth. Estrellita's sex rose then in vast angry threshing movements.

Peg leant down over the flesh throbbing above the saffron-colored belly. Her lips opened and then closed deliberately over the sex which kept moving upwards as if it would pull entirely away from the sand-colored testicles.

Estrellita spoke something in Spanish, the voice now at least an octave lower than when she spoke as Mr. Edward Hennings' spouse.

Later, back in her own room so seldom visited by Morpheus, Peg tried to clear her brain of what had occurred. Was it the strong perfume of the wild flowering jasmine which had in part driven both her and Estrellita to such abandonment or had she imagined the whole delirious episode?

Peg touched her lips still not entirely free of the effluvia of the youth who combined in her endowment the beauty of both sexes. She wondered if she would ever sleep again! Her whole past life receded away from her as if some earth tremor had swallowed it all up.

10

Mrs. Sawbridge's dining room was famous in its own right. It was so long it could easily seat fifty people. It was one of the few things Mr. Hennings had found to his taste in Manhattan.

He sat early this morning at the head of the table, and a stranger looking in might have assumed he was the pater familias. Ramon, the young Hispanic, was waiting on Mr. Hennings when Mrs. Sawbridge staggered into the chamber. Both Mr. Hennings and Ramon paused lengthily to stare at her.

Peg's appearance was so altered that no one spoke for a while. She was deathly pale, and gave the impression she had lost weight. Her hair, though beautifully marcelled, appeared dishevelled. But what was even more alarming was the wild expression in her pupils. She perfectly resembled one of the deranged female characters she was so famous for on the stage.

"My darling Peg," Mr. Hennings dropped his napkin and rose to help her to a chair across from where he had been seated. "What on earth's amiss!"

"My lifelong enemy, Edward, insomnia."

"I hope that is all," Mr. Hennings' concern for her touched Peg deeply at that moment. "You must confide in me, Peg, if you are worried about anything in particular." Turning his attention then to his hand-painted china plate, the old financier spoke in a more cheerful tone: "You serve the finest waffles I have ever partaken of."

Peg gave a forced smile. Her night with Estrellita kept coming and going through her brain, and always there remained the wonder if it had actually occurred.

"Is Estrellita," Peg began and then shocked by her own uttering the name of Edward's spouse, she halted.

"Is Estrellita what?" Mr. Hennings said. The kind light in his eyes wrung from Peg a poorly controlled sob.

"You surely can't be worried about *her*!" Mr. Hennings exploded in relieved laughter.

"I have been afraid, Edward darling, that she may not be comfortable here."

"Your concern touches me, Peg. But look here," he went on, chewing on a second helping of waffles, "you forget what that girl has been through! Would to God many young men had her stamina. She's seen three revolutions, a civil war, prison, where she was subjected to outrage after outrage, and finally marriage with me! She came through it all intact."

Peg coughed spasmodically, and rising abruptly Mr. Hennings patted his hostess gently on the back, and coming clear forward massaged her neck solicitously, and kissed her devotedly several times.

"Tell me a little of your marriage," Peg began when Edward had seated himself again. "I find it all so fascinating, Edward, your finding one another against a backdrop of insurrection and bombs."

Feeling more like herself, if not quite so strong as usual, Peg allowed Ramon to put a waffle before her. She tasted it and nodded approval to the young servant.

"We were married twice, to answer your query," Edward reminisced. "Ah, it seems so long ago. Once in Havana, and then again to make our contract binding, in Miami."

"I am very happy for you both, Edward. I am always happy in your happiness." Not daring to look at Edward as she spoke, Peg touched a huge sausage with her solid silver fork, and quickly put it in her mouth. Its deliciousness helped quiet her agitation for the moment.

Unaware of the convulsive emotions going through Peg's brain, Mr. Hennings continued: "Estrellita has a charmed life. I believe in fact she may be immortal. She comes, you know, from the finest Spanish aristocratic stock. She goes back in fact to royalty on her mother's side. Cuba, my dear, is largely half-breed like New York, but open any of Estrellita's veins and you'll find her blood comes from crowned heads."

"I recognized her quality, Edward, the moment you brought her here." Peg tried to appear her old imperturbable self, but her voice broke in short spasms. "However, I was not quite prepared for all her unusualness," she ended in a low whisper.

Mr. Hennings put down his fork. There was a queer change in his demeanor. "What do you infer from that?"

"Nothing, Edward, nothing. She entirely satisfies me."

Mr. Hennings picked up his knife and toyed with the waffle, then lifted a portion to his mouth and chewed thoughtfully. He wiped his thin mustache with the heavy linen napkin.

"Estrellita, Edward," Mrs. Sawbridge felt herself swimming out to deep water, "your wife, darling, is of a beauty so incomparable she could be taken either for a boy or a girl. Yes, such is her pulchritude." She motioned for Ramon to fill her waterglass.

Mr. Hennings considered this compliment by cocking his head to the left like a man enjoying the last notes of a string quartet. Then he smiled ever so faintly.

It was that faint smile that struck at Peg like revelation itself.

Mr. Hennings, she saw, did not know! She had probed him to the quick, and whatever his financial wizardry she took in his own innocence, naivete, yes, blindness, pitiful benightedness. He thought Estrellita was what she was not! He was Estrellita's husband in name only, and their relationship in actual fact must be as remote and formal as that between the Popes and the Swiss Guards.

49

The words from a Cuban song Estrellita often sang came back now to Peg as vividly as if the singer herself were present:

> Corazón, te adoro!
> Corazón, te pido!
> Corazón, te ruego!

Talking still in a kind of reverie although aloud, Peg intoned under her breath, "She is beautiful all over".

Edward Hennings appeared to go all to jelly at this compliment, and nodded again and again in gratification as he sometimes did when one of his prized possessions was praised by an expert.

"There is not a centimeter of Estrellita that is not either Adonis or Venus de Medici." Peg stopped after delivering this statement, for she felt at any moment she might throw caution to the winds and tell Edward all and everything. But looking square at Mr. Hennings now and studying his every motion and slightest expression, she saw with a kind of queasy unbelief that Edward got nothing from her words except the praise itself.

"He knows nothing," Peg came close to speaking aloud, and Ramon, sensing her agitation, lifted her coffee cup and filled it. Peg took Ramon's hand, held it, kissed it, pressed it with might and main.

"My dear friend," Peg gazed in the direction of Mr. Hennings, who was consuming his fourth waffle, "hear me, Edward! You are the luckiest man in the world. Fortune is enamoured of you, no question about it!"

Mr. Hennings gazed at his hostess, chewing contentedly. His monocle and his rings sparkled in the early morning sunshine.

11

After she and Estrellita had consummated their love, Mrs. Sawbridge went over the event day and night, hour by hour, minute by minute, and came to the very gradual realization that the young Cuban girl lived entirely in a realm of her own where truth or facts, even history itself were all mere shifting mirages to her. She supposed Estrellita had already forgotten Peg's impassioned lovemaking!

"She has seen too much for her age!" Peg more or less paraphrased Mr. Hennings' own explanation of the character of his wife. And Peg tried to imagine what the horrors she had lived through must do to flesh and spirit.

Often when passing Estrellita in the long dark corridors of her mansion, Peg would stretch out her arms and hold the youth to her and cover her precious features and breasts with wet kisses. She began to understand a part perhaps of Mr. Hennings' being deceived by Estrellita's sex. Like many young Cubans, Estrellita had developed her body by calisthenics and weights until her naturally flat male pectorals were rounder than many a full-grown girl's, certainly larger than the clothes-pins of the ballet. But Estrellita's pectorals, especially her nipples, were steel hard. They would never wither. Peg's lips and teeth found their way often to her bosom. She was reminded as she did so how Cleo had once pointed out to her mother that Peg had very strong lesbian

51

tendencies. Whatever the case, it was Estrellita's pectorals which drove Mrs. Sawbridge over the brink. She dreamed of those delicious mounds asleep or awake.

As if Mr. Hennings wished to torment all of them to the full, he arranged for Estrellita to play the Cuban flute for them in the evening and these galas on the part of Edward's wife made the youthful spouse a hundred times more fetching. Jared Wakeman, now, owing to queer remarks and winks from Peg, was more and more coming to a realization of Estrellita's true sex, and was consequently even more driven to distraction by the Cuban youth's extreme beauty as the latter puffed and blew on the flute. Estrellita's mastery of the instrument was astonishing.

After Estrellita's entertaining them with the flute solos, everyone departed with the exception of Mr. Hennings and Peg.

Mr. Hennings raised his right hand then – it was his way of telling those nearest to him he had something important to say. Peg held her breath for she still could not believe Mr. Hennings knew *nothing* where Estrellita was concerned.

"I know, my dear, it must be hard for you to fathom," the old financier began and Peg clutched her jade necklace as if to strangle herself with it. "You are still too young perhaps to understand my marriage," he went on. Peg closed her eyes and released her hold on her necklace. "I sometimes in fact think I am immortal, my dear, but I am not fool enough not to know that my own will to live is keeping me from the dark shore. My chief task now, if not my last, is to give you and Jared a theater. But you know that. And Estrellita's hand holds me to that task. *We are centuries apart*! I often say to her. And she, being born into nothing but cataclysms and catastrophes, I do believe understands! Her *hand* holding mine certainly understands!

"And, Peg, I have gone through not merely one stage of old age, but many! First there was green old age, hardly different from middle age. Then one progresses to puffing old age during which we no longer run up the stairs or leap out of bed on two feet, and after that debilitating old age in which one's eyes go bad, the bones creak and bend like meringue, but I am now, dear lady, at the stage where I count each breath I draw. And we come back to Estrellita...."

Peg opened her eyes wide now, her tongue appeared to form a syllable or two.

"*She* is my breath!" Mr. Hennings almost shouted. "I breathe only through her."

Again Mrs. Sawbridge felt driven from the shore. She was back where she had started: he knew nothing, nothing!

"Ah, yes, my darling Peg, so long as Estrellita is near me I cannot slip away into that dim shadow world. And then there is the theater I am planning for you and Jared. Estrellita and the theater! Hence I go on living. My real life is only through the grace of Estrellita! My mother, divine woman, my uncle (whom I adored to distraction) and my children by my first and second wives – they all look down upon me. I see them often as through a veil of Jared's cigarette smoke. But it is Estrellita who holds me to this world! After all, I suppose, she feels without me she would still be in a Cuban prison. Oh, Estrellita was naughty in Havana, no question about it." (He gufffawed loudly here.) "I don't excuse all the headstrong things she did. She cannot behave for long, granted. I've warned her about going down into the subways here with all her earrings and bracelets and gold necklaces, but Estrellita thrives on peril. You see, Peg, youth does not really believe there is death. And I had no notion of death myself until I was nearly seventy. It was only a word in the big black sticky newspapers.

"Edward, allow someone who also loves you dearly to disagree with you," Peg Sawbridge broke into his monologue. "Granted how important Estrellita is to you, how dear. But Edward, you need no one! No one in particular. You are a dynamo in your own right. A force of nature. You have not gone through all the varied stages of old age you just enumerated by grace of Estrellita. I really believe, Edward, you will never die."

53

"Peg of my heart," Edward Hennings appeared to melt all at once, "my dearest, how long have I known you? Fifty years or more?"

"Hush, hush, sweetheart," Peg beseeched him, "don't let Ramon and the other servants hear you go through the calendar! I must keep up some pretence at youth in my own menage! Ah, yes," she sighed at the thought of the years.

"We loved Chicago together, didn't we," Mr. Hennings interrupted, and rising came over to the Portuguese divan on which Peg was seated, and arranged himself beside her. "We were always thrilled by the nabisco-thin whiteness of the Wrigley Building, and the bridge that rose and fell over the Chicago River...."

"And the huge Blum's Vogue sign," Peg reminded him, "which one glimpses while being whirled to the South Side on the I.C. railway."

"It was sheer destiny which brought us together," Peg recalled her running into Edward on a cold snowy November night when she was so poor she could not afford a winter coat or proper shoes. Mr. Hennings had gone up to her and doffed his hat.

"May I be of some assistance to you, my child?"

They were in front of the Art Institute. As today, Mr. Hennings was dressed in fashionable expensiveness, but then he had *both* eyes to appraise his catches. They went off together then arm in arm in the snow. And despite all the vicissitudes which had come between them in the interim, her many marriages, his innumberable triumphs as an international financier, they had kept track of one another, until here they were decades afterwards sitting together on a divan.

Part Two

12

"Who in the dreary hell let you in?"

Desmond Cantrell, Jared Wakeman's roommate, or, better described, his soulmate, addressed those words to Mr. Edward Hennings, who was seated in Des's 46th Street flat, and had almost gone to sleep waiting for Des's return.

Desmond Cantrell already knew to whom he was speaking for Jared had expatiated at length on the character and achievements of the old financier Maecenas.

Mr. Hennings held up a very longish key, and hallooed, "With this! I don't know why they call them skeletons exactly. But nobody makes keys like *it* any more." He motioned for Des to examine the object. Des took the key in his hand and stared at it absentmindedly while his visitor proceeded. "It has let me in places I needed urgent entrance to in over twenty-one countries. Never fails.

"I don't know why," Mr. Hennings continued, yawning obstreperously, "why I haven't been allowed to meet you. Both Mrs. Sawbridge and your friend Jared have conspired, it would seem, to keep us apart. I hardly was allowed to know you existed!" He now took out his over-sized timepiece from his breast pocket and after staring at it through his monocle, he looked critically at Des as he would have at a client who had kept him waiting for an appointment.

"Mrs. Sawbridge," Edward Hennings began when Des had

seated himself on a small stool at the old man's feet, "Peg, that is, regards you and Jared as the Damon and Pythias of the day. Of course, being a woman, she is wolfishly jealous of your love for one another. She claims that she has been barred even from coming here to see you. And she affirms that for some years after Jared left his Cherokee Indian landlord, she did not know that Jared had been secretly living here with you."

"The trouble with Jared," Des Cantrell shook his head, and spoke now as he often did when all by himself or drinking in some off-limits saloon, "is he won't admit he is living with another fellow. He has this small-town shame of being close to another man. So he goes through the rigamarole all the time of pretending he loves women. He has told me time and again he loves Peg herself, and now he says he is smitten with your wife, Estrellita."

"Oh, everybody falls in love for a while with *her*," Mr. Hennings dismissed this charge with icy boredom. "But did he tell you Estrellita has for the most part ignored him except where social amenities at Peg's may require her to nod or smile briefly to him."

"I'm telling you, Mr. Hennings, what he pretends he feels, not what he actually feels."

"I can tell just by the way you speak of him that you have very intense feelings for the Thespian."

Des made a desperate attempt to prevent a sob escaping from him, but the sudden kindness in Mr. Hennings' voice brought on a few scalding tears.

"Now, now," Mr. Hennings comforted him, "don't let's waste precious salt tears over what can't be helped. You have a friend in me, Des. I was drawn to you even before you appeared by reason of the way you keep your apartment here. It is clean, elegant, and homey. Jared is oh so lucky to have you as his friend and pardon the frankness, caretaker."

"I have never loved anyone so deeply as I love Jared," Desmond spoke through hoarse emotion. "But I'm afraid love is all on my side, Mr. Hennings. He only loves the theater, though theater in his case is mostly in his head, for nobody knows of Jared as a Thespian outside of our own private theatricals."

"That will be changed, Desmond, especially now I have met you. I intend to provide Jared and of course dear old Peg with a theater they can call their own."

Desmond gulped down more emotion and then reaching out took Mr. Hennings' weatherbeaten and heavily veined and ringed hand in his and kissed it gratefully.

"You are a kid after my own heart," the financier said. "I hope you've forgiven my forced entry into your domicile." In return for Des' show of affection Mr. Hennings kissed the young man paternally.

"The sufferings one endures in love," Mr. Hennings reflected. "I understand it all. I have lived through Love's pains for nearly a century, and I am still not immune from the stings of his arrows ... Des, we will be the best of friends. Always count on me. And keep this in mind. Jared deeply loves you in return. You are his only love, as Estrellita is only mine. He may be unfaithful to you as the clock moves its hands, but in the end it is you who occupies his heart and soul. So give up your sorrowing, Des, and accept Jared as he is, a stage-struck often headstrong boy with a vile disposition, but under his many faults, he has a true heart. He loves you."

"If I could only believe that," Des almost whimpered. "But it's good to hear what you say, Mr. Hennings, even if it's only words. If I won't offend you, I must say you yourself are something of an actor. Certainly an orator."

"My mark in the world if mark I have made, Des, is that I have had to persuade, influence, and enlist to my banners people in many countries of the world. And so I have learned to show them now and again how to conduct their own lives. You, however, Des, have won me to you as much or more than Jared. But that is because I regard you both, as I think poor Peg does also, as two youths knit together with one soul. You two boys are *one* in my eyes!"

Desmond moved his head gratefully and looked at the floorboards.

"I want to believe you, Mr. Hennings. That Jared loves me, I mean. For he is all I have now, as my father has all but disowned me because of my strong feelings for Jared, and for my being, as Dad calls with scorn, also a Thespian."

"I am surprised in this illiterate town people know the word, 'Thespian'. I myself have barely heard it on anyone's lips since my own youth when of course English was spoken even by shop-boys and housemaids."

"But we need some refreshment, Mr. Hennings, don't we?" Desmond said as he opened a small cupboard and brought out a dusty bottle of something.

"I want you to taste this apple brandy from the Basque country, Mr. Hennings, and as a toast to your Estrellita."

Mr. Hennings smiled benevolently and took the small glass from Desmond Cantrell. Drinking from another, even smaller glass, the young actor toasted his visitor: "To skeleton keys when they usher in an intruder like you, Mr. Hennings!"

They drained their individual glasses at the same time, after which Mr. Hennings took Des in his arms, hugged him a long while and gave him kiss after kiss of goodbye, but with the parting adjudication: "This is only the promising beginning of our very special friendship, Des!"

13

Edward Hennings was not faithful to his Estrellita. It never crossed his mind on the other hand that she was capable of real unfaithfulness to him. He had saved her from so many horrors, of which physical pain was the least important, that he was convinced all she required in this life was the certainty he was nearby guarding her, keeping her safe from the "militia" as she called all external danger threatening her. So long as Edward Hennings was there, she required no other assurance, for what did clothes, food, or a roof over her head matter if her protector were not to be within earshot.

Edward's excursions with young men or sometimes girls, his fleeting infatuation with a new face, all these mutabilities Estrellita was aware of, but they flitted in and out of her consciousness. Even when she opened the door on her husband's lying beside some naked young man or girl, her jealousy was not actively roused. After all, Edward had not saved any of *them* from the jaws of infamy and death! Edward was to her mother and father as well as husband. Whatever he did, so long as he was her protector, was inconsequential. Had she never met him that time in Havana, she would today (the thought came to her a thousand times a day) be something seagulls might disinter from the soaked shore.

On the other hand, Edward ignored her own unfaithfulness. Actually he did not look upon what she did as unfaithfulness, for when he in his turn opened a door and saw her lying in the arms of an admirer, it only confirmed him in his pride that he possessed so beautiful a wife. He closed the door and sighed with the happiness of the proud possessor of a treasure.

Detest though he did present-day Manhattan and the boroughs of which she was queen, he found a few things to solace him since the fall of Old Havana. His greatest happiness now came when he chose to ride in one of the horse-drawn carriages stationed near one of the more palatial hotels. Edward rented the carriage usually for the entire day and evening, though he often brought his ride to an abrupt halt when he caught sight of a youth of his fancy.

Tonight, Edward ordered the driver to take one of the less-frequented routes, much to the chauffeur's protests on the grounds that they might meet danger if they went in that direction.

In reply, Edward Hennings listed all the *really* dangerous episodes of his life in most of the continents of the world.

The road down which they were ambling was deprived of street lights or any other illumination, a purposeful oversight according to the driver on the part of the crooks in city hall. Then all at once, as if from nowhere, their carriage was lit up by countless torches held aloft by half-naked young men, who shouted and bellowed at Mr. Hennings and his driver. They held banners and signs, some of which Mr. Hennings could read:

> Save our gifted Youth from the Plague!
> Redemption Now!
> No More Deaths without Retribution!
> The Secret Government Decrees our Deaths!

To the loud protests of the carriage driver, Mr. Hennings insisted on getting out of the cab. He had not proceeded very far toward the crowd of young men with the torches when he caught a glimpse of his driver turning around briskly and then making off at breakneck speed back toward the city.

"Good riddance," Edward shouted after the departing carriage.

"Thank God, you've come at last," one of the half-naked young men went up to Edward and kissed him on the mouth. "We feared you would never make it. Please come with us."

Mr. Hennings, unlike many men of his social class, because he had been through what Mrs. Sawbridge called vicissitudes was not unduly taken aback by such a greeting. And in any case, what he feared more even than death was boredom. The torchlit men, their state of undress, and his having been dumped by his carriage driver gave him an enormous lift and a swirling rush of energy.

To Edward's considerable satisfaction, he was ushered into a large, even monumental building, lit by gaslight and spacious enough, he thought, to be the kind of theater Jared and Peg might require for their theatricals. Despite his weak protests that he was not a public speaker, he was led up to the stage itself, on which twelve young men were seated, all holding papers, which he presumed were either their "parts" or their prepared speeches.

To Edward's supreme gratification, one of the seated young men leaped up and embraced him. It was Desmond Cantrell!

"Why, I'd swear we only just now parted," Mr. Hennings returned the young man's embrace.

"Sit here beside me," Des invited him.

"But where are Peg and Jared?" the old adventurer wondered.

"Peg and Jared back our movement, Mr. Hennings, only surreptitiously. Especially Jared."

Mr. Hennings had been away too long to know exactly the total extent of the Pest or the Plague.

Even Des Cantrell was a bit incredulous at hearing that his new-found friend was largely in the dark about the greatest cataclysm to afflict youth of genius and promise, but then going over in his mind again Edward's having undergone revolutions, civil wars, mutinies, and natural disasters, the younger man gave him a clasp of absolution and forgiveness.

All the while Edward had been escorted up the interminably long aisle which led to the stage he had been detained by youths who gave him leaflets describing the crisis of the Plague, and others who whispered into his ear their own private disasters, so that by the time he reached the platform itself, he was fairly well informed as to what had been going on for the past few years. The Plague only highlighted in his own mind the total collapse of New York itself.

Because of Mr. Hennings' extreme age and the general weakness of his legs, two of the most robust youths in the audience volunteered to stand on either side of him in case he should totter. Mr. Hennings then delivered his speech (or oration) which came to be known as "We are the Last Frontier."

In an eloquence almost never heard in what Mr. Hennings called "these mealy-mouthed times" he reviewed his own long life and his isolation because of his love of manly comrades and perfect masculine friendship.

Cries of ecstatic agreement came from all throats, especially "We are the last frontier!" from the balcony, largely occupied by young men under the legal age.

EDWARD HENNINGS' ORATION

Wetting his lips generously and adjusting his eyepiece, the old financier began in a strong, if shaking, voice:

"I am speaking to you, young men from another century, and a long exile from my native land. But we have one thing in common. We are bonded together by our love of comradely affection, and manly friendship and devotion. Time and age therefore are powerless against such love."

Here there was thunder-like applause and vociferous gruff cries of approval and encouragement. The roof and rafters of the ancient building (condemned and then abandoned by the politicians years ago, along with a luminous-watch-dial factory) gave back echoes, reverberations, and finally crashing sounds as if the whole edifice was about to collapse about their ears, and sink into the ground.

"Our comradely affection for one another," Mr. Hennings' voice bravely rose above the din, "has been scorned and threatened always by a corrupt government and church, shoddy lickspittle press, and the brain-shampooed populace. We have know throughout history only opposition, contumely, persecution, and isolation. Therefore, we, of all people, cannot now be dismayed for long by the virus of pest or plague. We have too intimately known the virus of the power of state and church, directed against us and aided by the venal and coprophagous press and *hoi polloi* of the mob!"

Mr. Hennings spoke a few other words but what he said was drowned out entirely by ear-splitting cries of approval and admiration. The old financier sat then, or rather, collapsed in the chair beside his new friend, Des Cantrell, who leaned over to embrace and kiss him, but the applause was so overwhelming, Mr. Hennings had to rise again and again to acknowledge the acclaim until at last he gave an extravagant bow, down almost to his polished, lacquered boots in a manner grand opera stars might envy.

"We shall soon see a theater – if there is breath in my body – dedicated to every youth who wishes to be free!"

Then, to Edward Hennings' gratified surprise, Des Cantrell rose and delivered the principal speech of the evening. But the contagion of residual enthusiasm for Mr. Hennings was still so rife that applause continued to rise every few minutes, making inaudible most of what Cantrell was saying.

Even had Mr. Hennings been able to take in Des Cantrell's speech (and he realized it was a beautifully prepared one), the sight of so many handsome men in the flower of their youth united here by a common purpose and destiny, diverted the old Maecenas' attention from anything else. He felt he had at last left the mean-spirited present and gone back to some classical eon of divine fellowship and trust and flawless and ideal affection.

65

14

"Cantrell! Cantrell! How could you do such a thing. I ask you!"

Mrs. Sawbridge was surrounded by a stack of newspapers whose front pages blared in headlines the mass meeting at the Amphitheater with oversize photos of Mr. Hennings kissing Des Cantrell. She was even more taken aback, however, by Des' cool composure. He and she were, she reflected, rivals, after all.

Des sat down without being invited to do so on the most comfortable of the newly upholstered settees, and without Mrs. Sawbridge's having instructed him to do so, Ramon poured Des a king-sized cup of coffee.

"How could you stab me in the back?" Peg went on. But the porcelain-like coloring of the young man's complexion and his good looks in general made her anger subside a bit. No wonder, she thought bitterly, Jared is so smitten by him. And no wonder he has kept Cantrell all to himself! For to hear Jared talk, he lived alone and neglected on West 46th Street, when here was the rebuttal to that lie, Cantrell himself, large as a fashion plate, drinking from her coffee cup, and seated as her guest.

"This is the last kind of publicity Mr. Hennings needs, Cantrell. Especially when he is on the brink of bestowing on us a theater. Now what will happen? Why on earth would you invite him to a public insurrection?"

Cantrell put down his coffee cup and stared at Peg.

"He wasn't invited, Mrs. Sawbridge," he spoke with poorly controlled anger and contempt. He resented her influence over Jared, and he was even more resentful of Jared's obvious affection for the older woman.

"Not invited, Cantrell, when all the press photos show you and Edward hugging and even kissing one another for dear life."

"As Jared has so often said, It's a pity Peg doesn't put as much umph in her acting as she does in her daily tiffs in her own domicile."

She was about to go on with her denunciation when Cantrell jumped up very much in the manner of Jared Wakeman, and shouted: "He appeared unbidden and uninvited and stumbled in at the Amphitheater, just as he stumbled unbidden and uninvited at my place. He entered my quarters with a skeleton key, for your info. But why is it, Mrs. Sawbridge, you never get your facts straight before you assume your role as prosecuting attorney, judge and jury?"

"You can't expect me to believe that Edward Hennings merely stumbled in on such a meeting uninvited and oblivious to what the meeting was about."

"That's exactly what happened. Besides, his excursions in his horse-drawn carriages have become fairly scandalous. I wonder, Mrs. Sawbridge, if you indeed know who Mr. Hennings actually is."

"I have known Mr. Hennings for at least thirty years."

"Then you should be aware of how often he stumbles in on all kinds of goings-on he is not invited to, with or without the aid of his skeleton key."

"Hard, hard to believe or swallow."

Vanquished, she sat down and nodded to Ramon to bring her more coffee.

"This is the first time you've had the courtesy even to invite me to your home," Cantrell went on, still raging, and she could see that Jared had in her visitor one of his most cultivated and brilliant pupils, for at that moment he was almost exactly like the Thespian, good looks, bad temper, cutting words and all.

"Then, if what you saw is true, accept my apology, dear Cantrell."

"I'll think about it," Des replied, and gave Ramon a quick wink.

"It does poor Edward no good to be photographed and written up as though his entire life was devoted to the cause of young male homosexuals."

She shook her head and her long string of beads moved in a rhythmic motion.

"I have known for some time that when the chips are down, it's you Jared gives his final allegiance to!"

"I wonder about that, Mrs. Sawbridge."

"Oh, for pity's sake, call me Peg, for you've broken my heart and so why then should formality be the order of the day."

"I think your heart is even harder to break than Jared's. You're both made of steel."

"I don't know more what I can do for you now than perhaps stoop down and kiss your boots."

"I can relieve your mind on one point however," Des Cantrell accepted a piece of banana cake from Ramon, "nothing can possibly spoil Mr. Hennings's reputation, for the simple reason he is above and beyond – reputation. I have only known him about two days, but in that brief space I have got by rote, I do believe, his strong points. And fear of press, public, or government, secret or open, are of no import to him whatsoever."

"Des Cantrell," Peg Sawbridge began in almost a prayerful tone, once Ramon had left the room. "The great, terrible fact is, we have been kept apart. I need not say, my dear, by whom. I have hardly been permitted to know you exist. Jared is secrecy himself. After all the hours and days I've spent with him, I know so little about him. Including the deep friendship you both feel for one another. Let me say this: I want also to be your friend. I want you to come and go as freely as Jared comes and goes. You do not need a skeleton key, dear boy. The doors to my home are open to you. Count me as your friend. Will you?"

They both rose at the same time. Well, why not, Cantrell muttered inaudibly. Weren't they both trained in histrionics by the same teacher?

Mrs. Sawbridge, never one to lose time, took Cantrell in her arms, and he caught whiffs of Toulouse toilet water, and an assortment of jewels and rings pressed hard against him. Her rain of kisses was not unwelcome at that moment.

"I want also to be your friend, Peg," the young man spoke throatily, and a few tears stood in his blue eyes.

"Then, this is only the beginning, dear Des," she kissed him on each of his eyes, "the overture of something very, very special for me, and I hope for you also. Forget any recrimination that escaped from me. I believe you, every word you have spoken. Mr. Hennings is a law unto himself. Furthermore, I minimize his greatness in implying *you* were behind his public spectacle."

It was Des Cantrell's turn now to take Mrs. Sawbridge in his arms.

Riding a day or so after his public appearance in the Amphitheater, in an even more ostentatious carriage, the spokes of whose wheels glittered with gold dust, dreaming perhaps of acacia trees and wild jasmine, Mr. Hennings' eyelids opened for a moment to take in a young runner, naked except for a cache-sexe, someone who looked familiar.

"Pull over in front of and halt that jogger!" Mr. Hennings gave his imperial order, and the driver, now used to the whims of his fare, did exactly as ordered.

When the runner made a motion as if to detour from the path blocked by the horse and carriage, Mr. Hennings seized the buggy whip and struck it again and again against the wheels.

"Get in at once, Mr. Wakeman! Do you hear?"

Jared stopped in his tracks, for of course it was the Thespian out for his physical conditioning, sweat pouring from every part of his body and threatening to drench completely the pathetic rag covering his pubis.

"I have a bone to pick with you or I wouldn't cut short my run," Jared got out breathlessly.

"It's too bad I didn't bring a whole cabinet full of Turkish towels," Mr. Hennings remarked, noting the pools of perspiration covering the leather seat and the floor of the carriage, once Jared had sat beside him.

"You have been putting ideas, I understand, in Desmond Cantrell's already over-impressionable brains!"

"There are many who say," Mr. Hennings spoke, in his contemptuous manner, poker-faced, "that the opposite is true, and he has turned me from being a theater Maecenas to a propagandist for his own cause."

"Mr. Hennings, get one thing straight, and we'll proceed smooth as silk. *I* am Desmond Cantrell's only cause. Any other banner he marches under espouses school-boy truancy."

"You all, Peg especially, speak like nineteenth-century melodramas."

"Don't meddle with my staff, Mr. Hennings," Wakeman went on. "Is that plain modern English for you. Keep your nose out of my affairs!"

Used to total obedience, Mr. Hennings felt a cool thrill of excitement at being dressed down and even insulted by the Thespian, especially since Jared was in line to benefit so largely from the old man's generosity.

By way of reply, Mr. Hennings chuckled delightedly.

"Skeleton keys, my foot, Mr. Hennings," the Thespian went on with his ill-tempered harangue. "You can barge in on old Peg, but mind your manners a little better at Des' and my establishment. We don't tolerate easily visitors impromptu. Clear?"

"I admire your tact and your *politesse*. I stand corrected, rebuked and put in the dunce's corner. After this, I'll call you for an appointment weeks in advance.

"Have a swig," Mr. Hennings produced a bottle of his favorite beverage, Vichy Celestin.

Without a word more Jared Wakeman drained the entire bottle at almost one swallow.

Then Mr. Hennings, like an actor or perhaps an acrobat in one of Jared's own melodramas, bent low and put his lips on the pearls of sweat on the Thespian's marble-colored chest.

Despite his long career as an actor and confidence man in general, Wakeman was considerably taken back at what he would later call "this outrageous public gesture."

Recovering from his amazement, Jared got out: "I am beginning to see, sir, why you have been driven out of every country on the globe!"

Refreshed from his drink off Jared Wakeman's solar plexus, Mr. Hennings spoke gravely and matter-of-factly: "The wonderful thing about your perspiration, dear Jared, is it is very lacking in strong saline properties. In fact, did I not know I was drinking from your breast-bone, I would say I was quaffing some of my own Vichy water."

Jared looked down at his calloused feet, and groaned, or sighed.

"I may have to tell Peg I have met my match," he turned and looked the financier square in the face. Then after some hesitation, he took the old man's ringed fingers, and pressed them. "You can have another drink any time I am in a lather, let me tell you, Mr. Hennings," and he kissed the old man's hand.

"But give an ear, sir," the Thespian shook his index finger at him. "You are my Maecenas. Get it? Mine, and mine alone. Don't get too cosy with my roommate, Des Cantrell. I won't have it. And don't join up with the Amphitheater crowd. It's the theater, Edward Hennings, that is your bounden duty and calling, not politics and the marches in the street of the war against the Plague. It's the theater where you're needed, sir. *My* theater. You belong entirely to me. You're mine, mine, mine. Oh, go ahead, kiss Des Cantrell all you want, who cares. He's under lock and key to me in any case. And hoodwink old Peg till she can't tell a cock from a hen, but you put your cream energy where I need you. I won't have any weak-kneed backsliding on your part."

Mr. Hennings' eyepiece fell to his rib cage, his mouth came wide open, showing an effulgent row of gold, and a very pink tongue emerging on his slightly rouged lips. He gazed in a kind of considerable awe and incredulity at the actor, wet from head to foot.

"I felt I had been sold at public auction," he later told Peg, "and that my new master was naked Cupid himself."

But before allowing Jared Wakeman to leave the carriage, Mr. Hennings gave out in a singsong some refrain composed of scraps of his collected wisdom:

> "Flesh and bones from earth!
> Moisture and sweat from water!
> Warmth from fire!
> Love against the grave!"

15

Des Cantrell had one thing in common with Edward Hennings. He was unfaithful to the one person whom he entirely, almost rapturously loved, Jared. Des would have sworn on the family Bible, if he could find it, that he was true to his "soulmate". And in a deep sense, this was true. But twenty minutes after swearing on holy writ, and after Jared had gone off to play-practice, and time hung heavily upon him, Des would shave, part his hair carefully, change his B.V.D.'s, and make a beeline to The Spent Candle, the most notorious saloon then in existence, and after a few drinks and a joint or so, he would amble back to the curtained back room illuminated only by what appeared to be a 7½-watt bulb.

Des's excesses, instead of making him look dissipated and hard of features, only bestowed upon him a more chaste and spiritual, if slightly wasted appearance. In fact, Des's growing ascetic look kindled, if possible, an even greater love in Jared's heart.

What neither of the young men even suspicioned was that Des Cantrell had contracted the Pest. They had felt the bacillus only chose others. Somehow they believed that their high realm would never be touched by such a sickness, that their own love kept them out of its reach. But there were times when Jared would look up suddenly and see something he did not understand in his lover's brow and mouth. The shadow he saw on Des's face would pass over to him, and then Des's sunshiney smile in return would banish any fear or suspicion. He would hold Des in his arms and abandon himself to loud kisses.

Jared's favorite composer was Richard Wagner, as his favorite writer was Friedrich Nietzsche. Des, on the other hand, had almost a horror of both Wagner and Nietzsche. His own favorite composer was Debussy, and he hardly ever read anything but a battered copy in fine print of the complete plays and poems of Christopher Marlowe.

Then, finally, upon some unspoken understanding between the two, Jared put away all his Wagner cassettes, and closed the pages of Nietzsche. He began to hear something in Debussy he had not found there before. An indefinable languor was stealing over Jared himself as he kept a kind of surreptitious vigil over his lover.

"What is it, Des?" Jared would sometimes whisper as he held his friend in his powerful arms. "Why can't you tell me, huh?"

"Don't have anything to tell, Jared" Des would always reply. "I've got you with me, haven't I? What more is there to tell?"

"But are you well, Des? I mean – "

"What do you mean, 'well'?"

"You're pale lately. And thin."

"Oh."

They pressed against one another silently.

"Do you know what the New York fire engines remind me of, Jared?" the younger man inquired during one of their reveries together.

"What, Des?"

"The Furies of Aeschylus."

Jared snickered.

"Why do they have to sound so loud, Jared?"

In a sudden spasm of fear, Jared touched Des's ears with his two hands, then he kissed his friend on each ear lobe. As he kissed his lover, Jared listened more attentively to the fire engines screaming down the street outside.

It came down on Jared like a skyfull of hailstones. He walked and walked, all the way from West 46th Street to Brooklyn. He had not realized, perhaps, why he was going in that direction, or who would listen when he got there, wherever *there* might be. Behind him, as he crossed the Brooklyn Bridge, the lights of the Manhattan skyscrapers appeared like the bits and pieces in a child's kaleidoscope.

Jared did not employ skeleton keys in the manner of Edward Hennings. He used a stout wire of his own fashioning to open the outside two doors of the St. Francis Retreat House. He walked up the two flights of carpeted stairs to the dormitory with the heavy, unsteady tread of an old man.

Brother Andrew was playing a dulcimer which a Lebanese had made for him a few years back. He was almost ashamed of the way he played so expertly on the instrument, but though against the rules of his order to play this late at night, the dulcimer solaced him in the long vigil of night when he could not sleep, and it was soft enough not to disturb the other brothers.

"You!" Brother Andrew whispered at the sight of Jared. "I suppose it's futile to ask how you got in. I know how close you are to the King of the Pit." Then, seeing his visitor was in a bad way even for him, Brother Andrew softened his tone. "Sit over there, Jared, before you fall flat on your handsome face."

Instead of sitting in the one guest chair, however, Jared threw himself on the brother's hard cot.

"I don't believe you've been drinking, or smoking something," Brother Andrew studied Wakeman. He touched two or three final notes on the dulcimer before putting the instrument away.

"Don't you remember, I'm the only member of the generation who doesn't do any of those things?" Jared mumbled.

"How many years have you been an actor and yet

three-fourths of the time you never open your lips wide enough for so much as a sigh to come forth."

Not even having heard the brother's reproach, Jared got out:

"Des has the Plague." The sentence came out as loud as a fire bell.

Brother Andrew rose from his tiny, broken, wooden chair and half stretched out both his arms, then let them fall lifelessly to his sides.

There was such a look of dismay on the brother's features that you might have supposed for a moment someone had slipped a mask over his face. The muscles of his throat moved convulsively and a thin film of spit spread over his mouth and chin, and on down to his well-defined Adam's apple, which rose then came up and down. Jared, gazing at the brother, thought he could see spiritual love.

"You wouldn't dare joke," Brother Andrew spoke aimlessly, and Jared could see only the whites of the brother's eyes.

But Andrew was only speaking perhaps to his own incredulity.

"And Desmond knows?"

"If he does, he puts the knowledge away in some deep hole in the ground. No, he don't know. I'm sure he don't."

"How far," Brother Andrew barely breathed now, "how far has it got?"

"Far, far," Jared watched the brother. "I think it may be close to the end. If you look away from him for a half hour and then look back he seems in that short time to have lost more weight, more color. His eyes are alive with the message!"

Brother Andrew wiped his lips now with a wad of something that resembled cheesecloth. He held the cloth in both his hands a long time before throwing it in the trash basket.

"This is the first time in all the years of our friendship when there's no trace of the actor in you. All that is you is coming straight out."

"Brother Andrew, watch out!"

"I always watch out when I'm with you, Jared," the brother smiled nervously, as the actor's features were distended in black anger. "I'm not afraid of you anymore."

"All right, rub it in. You see me down, and you can put your heel on my mouth and praise me for not play-acting as you twist the leather on my face. Go right ahead."

But all at once, without warning, Jared rose up and then threw himself down at Brother Andrew's feet. He held to the brother's legs, and made grotesque gurgling sounds.

"Save him, brother, save him."

Andrew's right hand fell mechanically on the crown of Jared's head. The scalp and hair felt hot to the touch, like a fevered mouth and tongue. Then the brother put his fingers through Jared's thick, abundant yellow hair, snarled here and there, and all giving out an electric current to his hand.

"Beside himself," Andrew thought bitterly.

Letting go of the brother's legs, Jared raised up his face, stained with tears and snot. "You have the gift to heal. You told me so once, long ago, when we were lovers. Maybe you don't remember by now we were in love! Or that you heal!"

"I'm afraid you have a higher opinion of my faith than I do, Jared." He bent down and kissed the actor on his brow.

"I know you can do something, brother. I know it or I would not have dragged myself over here at this hour."

All at once the piece of wire by which Jared had jimmied the locks of the retreat house fell out on the floor.

Andrew picked it up and stared at it. He smiled, and then Jared broke out in a kind of laugh, quickly followed by a kind of renewed sobbing.

"I realize now I can't live either if Des goes, brother."

"You said that about Moon Silverspoon before he died," Andrew reminded him. "And about Brad, too."

"No, no, they were not my all," the actor moaned and moved his head about in tiny circles.

"I can only do what I can do, Jared." Uneasily, he turned away now from Jared like someone who fears if he shows his back to the troubled person he will not find him again when he turns around.

Andrew went to a chiffonier and took something from the first drawer. Reaching then for a decanter of water, he poured a full glass from it.

"Listen to me, Jared. But get up off the floor first of all."

Andrew held the glass and the pill from the drawer of the chiffonier with a kind of bored patience like the priest extending the wafer.

"You need it," Andrew recommended, and he put the pill on the actor's tongue. "And some water." He extended the glass. Jared drank as thirstily as Mr. Hennings when pressing his mouth on Jared's bare chest.

"Did you swallow it?"

Jared nodded, and taking the brother's free hand, kissed it.

"Now go home, Jared. It won't look right if you spend the night with me."

"You'll say prayers for him, brother."

Andrew nodded.

"I forgot to bring any money with me," the Thespian said, like one coming out of a long sleep.

Andrew fished in his habit, and brought out some bills.

"You haven't changed a bit, have you, Jared? Always broke, and borrowing, always the little waif, looking for your next touch."

The brother realized Jared had not heard him, busy counting the bills.

"Pray, brother? Pray?" Two great silver tears stood in Jared's eyes. "Pray for me, maybe, too?"

As in times past when they had been lovers, Brother Andrew took Jared in his arms and held him with a pressure that was painful. Then, pulling away all at once, Andrew took his visitor's left hand in his, and opened it like a book to the scratched, soiled and worn palm and kissed the life line that was prominent there.

"There's hardly a ticking of the clock that I don't pray for all of you," the brother said, and kissed Jared goodbye on his lips.

But once Jared was gone, Andrew stood before the closed door for a long while.

He was wondering then if God heard him any longer. He was wondering indeed if God even wanted to hear him. He felt the heavy rock of unbelief over his heart. Around and about him, also, while his own face was still dewed with the kisses and tears bestowed on him by Jared Wakeman, he saw all at once the faces and tears of the young men who had recently gone down into the permanent night, struck by the same poison Des Cantrell suffered from.

Looking up, Brother Andrew saw himself in the small, partly cracked looking-glass above his cot. He was astonished at how young he managed to look, almost as young as Jared or Des.

"Yes, I will do something for you, Jared," he called out, as if Jared could still hear his voice. "I will do something for the boy you love."

He looked down at his strong farmer's son's hands. He looked at the crucifix on the wall.

"For the first time, Jared, you confessed on your knees you loved someone, and your tears washed and sealed your confession. Yet you don't know how blessed you are, do you, that love found you."

16

Edward Hennings had chosen as his rendevous with Madame Sawbridge (as he referred to his guest in front of the maître d'hotel) the most extravagantly expensive restaurant in the world. There had been a similar restaurant he reflected in Havana years ago, where eight waiters attended a single patron. And there, if four drops of water were drained from the thick cut glass, like lightning a serving man, wearing evening clothes even for breakfast, replenished the liquid, whilst in the later hours the bits of roast suckling pig were sometimes brought to one's lips by another special servitor who blew gently upon the morsel if he deemed it too hot.

On and on Mr. Hennings went, chronicling the vanished splendor of La Habana.

Seeing that Peg was woolgathering and fidgeting, he tapped with the solid silver knife decorated with a coat of arms on its shaft, against the rim of his water glass, thereby summoning three waiters. Again, he was reminded all over of the city on the blue Caribbean.

Staring at her bemused taciturnity, he coughed out: "I thought you claimed you were dying of grief, Peg. Yet I find you have a very robust appetite for your kidney pie."

Coming out of her reverie, Peg brightened. "I must preserve my strength for others, Edward."

Mr. Hennings put down his napkin and adjusted his eyepiece. "Peg, I warn you!" He gave her a grimace she had never seen on his features before. "Let me emphasize what I've already told you. If I save Jared's lover, Desmond Cantrell, Jared must belong only to me from here on down the road! I mean this!"

But his eye and mind were diverted by the sight of a huge gold bracelet on her left arm.

Without ceremony he pulled the bracelet from her arm, and laid it down with a bang on the tablecloth. Then, he looked at the ornament concernedly with his eyepiece.

"I'm surprised," he spoke loudly enough for all the waiters to hear them, "surprised, amazed, humiliated even, that you'd wear something as tawdry, if expensive, as this piece of gold on your arm, for what is, after all, a noonday repast."

He lifted up her hand and kissed it several times.

"But touching on Jared, my dear," Peg began breathlessly. "I don't exactly understand what you mean by saying he must be entirely yours."

"You are not quoting me correctly, love." Mr. Hennings had mellowed a little by reason of the red bubbly drink he was consuming.

"I thought, dearest, you said he must be yours."

"I think he already is that, Peg. What I am emphasizing is that you must not meddle or interfere with my relationship with him. You once called me imperial. Very well, supposing I am. I get things done if that is imperial, while others merely make plans and dream dreams. If I am to give Jared a theater – in which you will star also" (here Peg bowed low), "then he must be entirely available, at my beck and call. He must not be busy elsewhere."

"And what about Desmond Cantrell?"

"We will heal him!" Mr. Hennings had never been so lofty.

Peg tasted again the crust of her kidney pie.

"To summarize," Mr. Hennings interrupted and stole a bite of her pie on his fork and tasted it approvingly, "then as now

Jared will be entirely taken up with his duties to me."

"And Estrellita," Peg took the plunge, "where does she fit into all this?"

"Estrellita is married to me," he snapped. "What else can she expect? While Jared and I are totally taken up with the ramifications of theater, art, declamation! You do sometimes surprise me, my child, in your kind of blind obtuseness and assumed naivete!"

"Oh Edward, Edward, I am a naive. You certainly know that. You forget, dear love, I came from a tiny town in Montana. Perhaps you forget how we met!"

"Tell it me over again, darling, for the thousandth time for it's a story you at least never tire of." He put down his utensils and napkin and lay back in his chair like a patron of a string quartet waiting for the first notes of the piano and viola.

"Well, Mr. Hennings, as you recall it was a blustery November evening on Michigan Avenue, in Chicago, of course, in front of the lions of the Art Institute. I was wearing only a thin skirt and under it a paper thin teddy, white sandals, and very little else. I was down to my last cent. And behold, Edward, you came out of a long black limousine and doffed your hat to me!"

"And, Peg," Mr. Hennings, despite himself, was moved, "we have been madly in love with one another ever since!"

"At least I have with you, Mr. Hennings!"

"Don't boast now. It's one of your many faults!"

"I'm afraid, with your love for Jared and Estrellita, there's very little room in your heart for poor old Peg Sawbridge."

He took her hand again and kissed it wetly.

"No one can take your place in my affections, Peg. Don't you see I always in the end return to you?"

"But I get cold all over, Edward, when you say Jared must belong entirely to you."

"I can't help your getting cold, can I? Don't you want the theater? Don't you want Jared's dream to come true?"

She was far away, he saw.

"You spoke, though, of healing."

They exchanged long looks.

"I know of your accomplishment in botanicals, of course, Edward. I believe you even wrote a book on tropical herbs."

"I thought I told you I would heal Desmond."

The finality with which he spoke made her stare at him.

"I think if you healed Desmond, you would keep Jared in your coat pocket whenever you needed him."

"He cares that much about Desmond?"

"Care is no way of putting it. His life is in Desmond. If Desmond goes, Edward, we won't have any Jared to star in your theater."

"You're certain he is that close to him."

"They have the kind of love we only read about in old books. So, if you want Jared body and soul, heal his other half. Heal Desmond."

"I don't believe you think I can!"

Peg folded her napkin, and the waiter took away her serving of pie and put before her a large silver finger bowl.

"I know you are a wizard. I truly believe you can do anything you decide to do."

"You'll see then what I am going to do in Desmond's case. I can't lose my theater, after all, can I?"

Mrs. Sawbridge's expression of supplication stopped him from saying more for a lengthy while.

Then he brought their reunion to a close by saying, "Peg, I believe you want Desmond saved almost more than Jared."

17

When, a few years back, his mother lay dying, Jared Wakeman took her rosary from her already ice-cold fingers and put it quickly under his maize-colored sport shirt collar. Almost at once he felt a surge of something go through his entire brain and body. When he let go briefly of the beads he looked down at his mother's face. She was no longer there to be his unsleeping guardian, censor, and luckless guide.

Des Cantrell had taken the place of his mother, his father, and his three brothers, all of whom had died preceding his mother's death, his brothers in the war, his father in a hunting accident.

But when he realized that Des was going to leave him also, Jared had the feeling as he rode the subway back from Brooklyn after his meeting with Brother Andrew that his knees were turning to some kind of watery soup such as derelicts are fed in charity kitchens.

He took out the rosary now and kissed the beads. His memory of his mother's death came back to him with a kind of strangulating urgency. At that moment he slipped to fall down on the floor of the almost empty subway car, near the emergency cord. He gazed at the cord zealously.

Then – and he would swear to this forever afterwards – he saw looking in at him from the stained, cracked window of the train, Jesus himself. He looked like any young drifter of today. He called to Jared by name.

Some passengers who appeared from nowhere were helping him up from the floor. They offered to summon an ambulance.

"He was as real as you," Jared explained to them. "The Good Shepherd."

Then, coming out of his dream, Jared got up hurriedly. He held the rosary in his right hand tight. It was wet with something though he could not remember weeping. He rushed out of the subway car at the next stop, away from his samaritans.

"Jesus cured by means of the Holy Spirit," Jared heard himself speaking now to a group of passers-by on the corner of 10th Avenue and 45th Street.

He remembered reading somewhere that the Good Shepherd often appears to atheists and infidels like himself. Yet though he believed in nothing, he knew all at once in the heavy rain that was falling now that love had always believed in him, and though he had perhaps never loved wholeheartedly in return he was to see from this odd hour on that no matter what he thought he believed or did not believe, love had claimed him, and would never from this time forth let him go.

18

"Helloo, Jared! Got your nose in the clouds? Don't you know us?"

Hundreds of voices were calling him. He had walked all the way to Brooklyn to see Brother Andrew, but now he had walked nearly from one end of Manhattan to the other. He had gone three or four times to Des's apartment on West 46th Street. The door was open, and Jared, seeing no trace of Des, left it open. Why close it if Des was dead?

He searched on. Jared was so well-known in and around 11th Avenue because of his underground theater appearances that he was greeted on all sides.

His shoe laces had come undone, he was dripping with sweat from head to foot. People thought he was on drugs.

"If Des," he said aloud, "if you, Des, are passed over, I will join you. I won't go on here another hour. If Des...."

The last place he expected to find Desmond was Peg's, because Peg and Des both pretended the other did not exist.

But where else was there to look?

He stood at Mrs. Sawbridge's open door, waiting like a delivery man. Inside, Mr. Hennings was speaking to an assembly of persons: Peg, Cleo, Estrellita, a few others. Their forms shut out from Jared's view the bed on which Des Cantrell was lying.

A cry like a military challenge from Jared brought all their attention to the newcomer.

Jared walked over to the bed on which his friend was stretched out. After gazing unbelieving at Des, he looked up at Peg and Mr. Hennings with a queer inquiring look.

"He's a little better," Mrs. Sawbridge took Jared by the hand and urged him to chair. "The crisis is past," she added dryly.

Despite his state of general numb stupefaction, Jared took his eyes away from Des long enough to realize that a quarrel of unusual acerbity and heat was taking place between Mrs. Sawbridge and Edward Hennings. Jared had never seen Peg so angry.

"You have no right to run down America the way you have been doing in my home, Edward. It is, after all, your native land! And look how you've profited from being an American!"

Mr. Hennings laughed just like the villains in the last century melodramas Jared and Peg occasionally selected from their minor repertory.

"And you have raved and ranted whilst this dear boy is lying at the point of –." Here Peg checked herself and as she gave a hurried glance at Jared. "I have never heard such rot coming from a mature man," Peg went on. "Saying that the Statue of Liberty has only welcomed riff-raff to our shores, that she is the Goddess of Scum!"

"I only say, Peg, what everybody knows but dares not breathe!"

"That all our Presidents and the mayors of all our cities are crooks and secret agents of hidden powers. I can't bear it, I can't bear it. You know better!"

She advanced toward Mr. Hennings and might have struck him had not Cleo intervened and guided her mother to the other side of the room, patting her on the back like an infant, and uttering soothing words of affection, followed by dry little pecks of kisses.

87

"If he thinks such things," Peg proceeded, "why can't he keep them to himself. You have always been a Bolshevik!" Peg raised her voice and glared across the room at Hennings.

The quarrel was a kind of relief to Jared's nerves. It made him a little more able to bear the sight of Desmond pale as calla lilies stretched out so motionless, so fearfully still.

"And where are the botanical remedies you promised us, and the potions you claimed would cure our dear Desmond!" Peg raged on and on.

Turning to Jared who showed only the whites of his eyes as he looked nowhere in particular Peg kept on! "You must pardon us, Jared, dearest, for engaging in an argument about as dignified as a wrestling match, but Edward has driven me to to distraction. He claims my house is bugged and that agents of the secret American government which rule the U.S. of A. are waiting inside and outside! And more and more! When all our attention should be given to dearest Desmond. And what is worse, Jared, are you listening, my darling? I am bounden to Hennings from early girlhood, don't you see, for my life and my career, such as they are. He possesses me!"

"You owe me nothing, you fool," Edward Hennings taunted her, and welcomed Estrellita now to sit on his knee. "What I gave you was given with no strings attached to it. And I have tried to get in a word edgeways during your patriotic rigamarole about the beauty of these United States. I gave and give you may word, that I will cure your boy over there, Desmond Cantrell, if you quiet down and let me work in my improvised laboratory."

"It is true, Jared," Peg was a bit calmer and kept clasping Cleo's hand in hers, "yes, he knows botanicals, and has set up a true tropical medical lab in one of my empty apartments.... But," she turned her fury again on Edward, "how dare you claim that I have allowed secret U.S. agents to tap my home in order to catch you at espionage! How could I betray a man who rescued me so long ago on a snowy Chicago street. For God's sweet sake, you ought to apologize on your knees!"

Edward's only reply was to kiss and hug Estrellita.

"Emancipated as Mrs. Sawbridge is in sexual and personal matters," Edward Hennings called over to the bowed form of Jared Wakeman, "she is as gullible as a schoolgirl for all the lies put out by the press, the White House, the preachers and the cardinals. She has swallowed the whole myth of America as the savior of the world, when even a schoolboy who had visited the public library ten or twelve times knows that we have not heard a word of fact or truth about our government and her leaders for two hundred years! But ...," and here, unceremoniously almost dropping Estrellita to the floor, Mr. Hennings hurried over to where Jared had collapsed over the prone form of his idol, Des Cantrell.

Shaking Jared almost painfully by his shoulder, Mr. Hennings went on, "You have got to believe in me. I cannot go into the laboratory and fetch out my botanicals if you are going to act like you are attending a wake." He slapped Jared smartly across the face. "Be like your surname, Jared, wake! I have cured many dread diseases, many! The Pest is no match for what I can do. But you must look alive, do you hear?"

Oddly enough, Jared lifted up his face and smiled, and took Mr. Hennings' weatherbeaten, gnarled hand and kissed it. "If you save him, Mr. Hennings, I will follow you to the ends of the earth. You know that, and I believe you. I believe you can save Des and save me!" Jared began to rise on speaking this but Mr. Hennings gave him a push back to a seated posture.

The old financier beamed, and then, taking Estrellita's arm in his, they exited on their way to the improvised laboratory.

"Edward, Edward!" Mrs. Sawbridge cried and hurried after the retreating Maecenas and his Estrellita. "I cannot let you part from me in anger. Forgive my harsh words, for heaven's sake." She tried to embrace the financier, but he moved slightly away from her. "If you cure Desmond -"

"*If*, you goose!"

"I believe, too. I am a believer. Edward, if you cure my dear Des, I will not only follow you to the ends of the earth, I

89

will go down to hell itself with you! And, Edward, oh tarry a little. Edward, I will even embrace Bolshevism if you cure this dear boy."

Mr. Hennings smiled in spite of himself.

"I hope the bugs in your mansion didn't pick up your last statement, Peg."

He bent down and kissed her.

"You are everything to me, Edward, you know that."

"Now let me prepare the antidote for our young invalid," Mr. Hennings implored her. "For even if Desmond were to breathe his last, a little flower from Santiago de Cuba will bring him back to us." Taking Estrellita by the hand, he broke out of Mrs. Sawbridge's firm embrace.

Peg went on standing at the threshold over which Edward and Estrellita had gone, when all at once Estrellita reappeared with a large tumbler of spring water, and carrying in her open hand two pastilles.

"Edward wants you to take these pills, Mrs. Sawbridge."

Peg kissed Estrellita warmly on the mouth.

"Mrs. Sawbridge would gladly take hemlock if it were offered by your hand, my sweet," Peg told her, and seized the tablets, put them on her tongue, and then drank the entire tumbler of water in almost one swallow.

"I wouldn't care at all if it killed me," she announced to everybody in the room. "But give an ear! I believe Mr. Hennings may be speaking the truth. Our entire world is foundering about us! Even the heavens, they say, are cracking in two over our heads." Quieting down, perhaps through what she'd swallowed, Peg grasped Estrellita then and held her in a loving embrace, and Estrellita hugged and kissed her devotedly in return.

Calm and order had barely established themselves in the room after the financier and his spouse had left when a fierce knocking on the door brought everybody to attention again.

Unbeknownst to all and against Mr. Hennings' firm instructions, Mrs. Sawbridge had summoned the noted medical expert and sometimes coroner, Blissett. She had nearly forgotten her deception. She recognized the banging on the door was coming from the doctor's heavy walking-stick which he carried to defend himself against muggers.

Summoning up the little courage she still possessed, Peg opened the door on the doctor. He embraced her so effusively almost everyone realized he was in an advanced state of intoxication.

"I've left a whole ward of patients to answer your bidding, my beloved Peg," the doctor cried, waving his heavy walking-stick in the air. "Meet my assistant, Mrs. Sawbridge," and the doctor pointed to a thick-set young man whose left eye turned markedly inward so that one did not know at whom he was looking.

Drunk as he was, Dr. Blissett did not take long to see that Desmond Cantrell was far past any medical assistance. For form's sake alone he sat down on the huge sofa on which the young man still lay immobile and felt his pulse, and used a stethoscope to probe his chest, and bathed Des's brow with a medicated cloth, handed to him by an assistant who had stolen in almost unnoticed. Dr. Blissett gave the cross-eyed assistant a queer, prolonged look as much as to say: "What are either you or I doing here, and shan't we leave at once?"

Dr. Blissett folded his arms, and shook his head repeatedly. Pulling out a legal-sized document from his jacket pocket he motioned for the assistant to begin filling the papers preparatory for his signature.

"But what have we here?" the doctor now took notice of Jared, who had slumped down on the floor beside the motionless form of Des. Hardly bothering to examine Jared any further, the doctor brought out from his black bag his equipment for such cases, rolled up the survivor's sleeve and was about to give him an injection when Jared appeared to rally and rose as his old surly self.

"I want to feel the full measure of grief," Jared shouted. "I don't want to have what I feel deadened or soothed or made nothing in the style of today! I want agony and hell!"

Having astonished, if not frightened the doctor by his

outburst, the Thespian walked off into one of the adjoining rooms.

Peg's own mental process was in so confused a state by now, that she was hardly aware the doctor had made his exit after handing her a death certificate, which she held unread in her hand like a fan. She finally was aware that Edward Hennings had entered the room and was contemptuously perusing the legal looking document which he had torn from her hand.

"What have you done," he began, after his perusal, in his bitterest tone. "Gone behind my back and called in some quack coroner from City Hall?"

"Des is gone, Edward, let's not have an altercation now!"

"You idiot, gone, tommy-rot, he's only in a dead faint."

Estrellita entered now with a small hand-woven basket containing various pink, pale lavender and crimson flowers whose names were unknown to anyone perhaps but Estrellita herself.

"Doctors have sent many a poor soul to his grave when their patient was only in a very deep slumber, my dear." Peg heard Edward's pronouncements. Jared had come back into the room, and, bending over, kissed her.

"She will meddle, and this time," Edward began speaking to Jared, "this time she has nearly sent poor Des Cantrell to the black shore!"

Sitting down beside the still form of Desmond Cantrell, Mr. Hennings lifted up the left hand of the youth, and proceeded to orate: "Desmond Cantrell dead? Look at his life line, would you." He turned all his fury on Peg Sawbridge.

Edward Hennings gazed dreamily down at Desmond. He brushed back a strand of the young man's yellow hair and smoothed it into place. Then to Peg's confused, wandering attention, she saw Mr. Hennings removing all of Desmond's clothing with methodical, almost bored ease. Before she could take it all in, Desmond was lying mother-naked, a kind of grim smile on his lips, a smile that had not been there before.

"If you'll stop your infernal blubbering, Peg, we'll have the boy up and taking biscuits and tea with us in no time!"

What followed then was to give Mrs. Sawbridge thoughts for her insomnia and material for conversations for months, years, decades to come, if decades were possible in her calendar.

Peg's eyes saw Mr. Hennings raise a kind of small, very thin knife and stab Desmond over his heart again and again. Her eyes saw this manoeuver, that is, but her mind did not believe what she saw, or what then followed. For, after the stabbing, her pupils focussed on Mr. Hennings' magician-like hands placing the petals of the flowers Estrellita had brought, into the young man's mouth, and, turning him over like a bundle of straw, he put more petals in his rectum as one would prepare a bird for the roasting oven.

Mr Hennings put his ear to Desmond's heart and listened carefully. Then, lifting up his head, he grinned triumphantly at Peg.

"His ticker is going it like a fire engine!"

Edward Hennings plunged his hand over the young man's chest with such force everybody thought they heard his rib cage crack. Lifting Desmond then up into his arms, Mr. Hennings went on babbling and orating in the loud manner Mrs. Sawbridge described as "preaching to the choir". And then, as much to her horror perhaps as her wild joy, she watched the dead young man choke and squawk and cry like a new-born infant being cut from his mother and brought breathing to life. The deadly pallor left Des's face, throat and breast, his sky-blue eyes opened wide, dripping a few fat tears. He yawned, broke wind, scratched his temples, and then laughed uproariously, gleefully.

If one had entered unexpectedly he might have thought everybody was at camp meeting in some river port, for there was nobody who was not rejoicing and praising providence for what had happened. Jared threw himself into Des's arms, and he was followed by Peg's bathing the newly awakened with her uncontrollable sobs and kisses of happiness.

"Our boy lives!" Mr. Hennings, with condescending,

contemptuous manner, allowed each and every one in the room to embrace and kiss his charge. Desmond even spoke a few unintelligible throaty words, and then lay back in his restorer's arms.

"Desmond Cantrell, dead!" Mr. Hennings kept repeating. "Never while I will live. Desmond shall live another hundred years, mark my word! Just listen to his heartbeat now! Draw close, all of you! Yet you, Peg would have risked his young life by admitting to your home a City Hall coroner, or sexton, or whatever he's called, who is not only a crook, but is deaf as an adder, and his cross-eyed assistant is in the last stages of softening of the brain. I hope you checked on your valuables before the pair exited, for the doctor is a kleptomaniac, and his assistant is a common sneak-thief. The doctor would pinch anything, like a crow, that glistens or glitters. So, ladies, look to see if you still have your bracelets and your rings and necklaces."

"All lies, lies," Peg cried in mock reproof, for her happiness at seeing Desmond alive made anything she said sound like "Hosanna, hosanna."

She turned to see Mr. Hennings tearing up the death certificate.

"Edward," she admonished very gently, "shan't your tearing up a legal document get us in difficulties?"

"Get us in difficulties? What on earth do you mean? To sign a certificate that someone is dead when he is *alive*? The doctor, if doctor he be, is in legal difficulties, my dear." Here Mr. Hennings kissed Desmond on the lips and hugged him, and to the wonder of all, including Mr. Hennings, Desmond put down one foot after another and rose with only some minor difficulty, and then fell back into the arms of his savior.

Estrellita handed Desmond a blue iris, which he smelled appreciatively.

Mr. Hennings rose now in the forensic manner he had displayed at the Amphitheater, and everyone was silent.

"Now the real task begins, gentlemen and ladies," he began. "It may prove easier to banish death than to rout the

Pest or Plague. But I am not daunted!" He turned to nod at Desmond, who returned a broad smile. "Many of you, including dear Peg, whom I adore, but who is a goose, you may think of me only as a Maecenas with special reference to my theatrical undertakings. But what many of you do not know is that after I tired of Swiss and international finance, I came to study, in depth, botanicals, in Santiago de Cuba. With Estrellita at my side!" Here he threw kisses in the direction of his spouse. "We two together discovered things not dreamt of since Galen. The Reds, as Peg calls them, gave me every encouragement! I even one time cured the Great Leader in Havana of a troubling malady. And now I am ready and eager to rid the community of the last vestiges of the Pest so that the bloodstream of our young men will circulate pure and undefiled."

All eyes rested on Desmond Cantrell, who had followed every word of his restorer with feverish attention and approval.

There would probably have been rejoicing and gaiety the rest of the day and evening if something had not then occurred, an event so discommoding that Mrs. Sawbridge wondered if she were not having one of the nightmares which interrupted her long hours of insomnia. For at the moment of their greatest happiness, the broad doors to her parlor were thrown open, and streaming in with their night sticks brandishing and their revolvers drawn were the police and some plainclothes men, and an official or two.

"Bluecoats, bulls, God in heaven!" Peg cried, and raising her hands in a gesture to forbid entry to the throng of police. They pushed her aside as if she had been side curtains to one of her antique cars.

Open-mouthed, she saw them go up directly to Mr. Hennings and Estrellita, heard them pronounce half-aubible statements such as "We arrest you, Edward Hennings, and your spouse of criminal conspiracy for violating the laws of this city," etc., etc.

"You shall not take him!" Mrs. Sawbridge intervened at the

same time she heard the handcuffs click on the extended wrists of Edward and Estrellita.

"In my house, never!" Peg vociferated.

"If you want to join them in jail, madame," one of the older cops warned her, "just continue with interfering with our bounden duty," and he threatened her with a new pair of handcuffs.

"Edward, my love, you cannot leave us like this," Peg Sawbridge cried after the retreating figure of Mr. Hennings. "You are my life and my prop against every vicissitude of life, my dear.... You cannot go out like this."

Mr Hennings turned then and half raised his manacled hands to her.

"Consider it, Peg, only as an interrugnum if you like. Estrellita and I will be back in no time! Mark my words. And we will, on our return, have a proper celebration of Desmond's coming back to us from the other shore.... And remember, my work has only begun. The removal from the bloodstream of our young men of the poison of our world, the punishment and tyranny of our venal government!"

Mr. Hennings' arresting officer pulled him violently away then, and the door closed on all the police and their captives.

19

"If I were not a life-long member of the Ornithology Institute, I would fetch my late husband's rifle and shoot every one of those damned mourning doves cooing on the eaves!" Peg Sawbridge uttered this malediction as she accepted from Ramon another pure Irish linen handkerchief for her to blow her nose on.

Days, endless days, like weeks or months, had passed since Mr. Hennings' arrest, and Peg had hardly moved from the windows facing the street. She kept her post as sentinel perhaps because she felt her presence at the window might hasten his return.

"Yet, Ramon," Peg went on, holding the servant's free hand in hers, "may the Good Shepherd forgive me for my damning the doves. I'm sure He was partial to mourning doves. And they are among the most beautiful of our birds. But that note, Ramon, that plaintive, unending cry! What, after all, do doves have to complain about? I am the one who should be out there on the building ledge moaning and sorrowing. Yet," here Peg rose treading painfully as she did so on Ramon's thin shoes, "God may punish me for not being forever grateful that our Des has been brought back from his terrible journey from the other shore. For you know, Ramon, as well as I, that Desmond Cantrell died and left us until our

97

miracle worker fetched him back. And to think such a savior has been put under arrest."

Mrs. Sawbridge then left the refectory, and took herself slowly to the front parlor where Desmond Cantrell lay on the same cushioned divan on which he had died some few days before. There was now a wonderful flush of color on his cheeks and throat, emphasized in part by the crimson shirt Peg had given him. But the truth was, she noted with a feeling of uneasiness, that he had looked more handsome when he had lain motionless and still and crossed over.

Peg bent down and kissed his satin lips.

"I do believe, Desmond, that I love you more than I do Jared."

"Watch that tongue of yours," she heard Jared's warning from across the room.

"But Jared, that was only hyperbole!"

"Hyperbole, hear her!" Jared sneered.

"Jared," Mrs. Sawbridge began her apology uneasily, "We must not quarrel after the miracle our lord has vouchsafed us. You have never been on so long a journey as Desmond, remember."

Jared was about to dispute perhaps the accuracy of Peg's assertion, but Peg hurried on:

"I foresaw all of this, Edward's arrest, a long time ago. Marvelous as he is, his ideas are, to put it mildly, dangerous, pestiferous! He speaks as he has always spoken, like a Bolshevik, and here he is, a billionaire probably many times over. But he is against everything! And so the authorities have got wind of it, and taken him into custody."

"Tommy-rot, Peg, to quote you," Jared flared up.

"Then why has he been taken away in handcuffs?" she wailed.

"Did it ever occur to you, sweetheart, that Mr. Hennings may have staged the whole thing? That the cops were extras? Remember, Edward Hennings is, in his own phrase, an actor manqué."

"Then I suppose, according to you, Jared, Des never visited

the other shore either, and was only awakened by Edward Hennings from a nap."

"Oh, those confounded birds will drive me mad!" Peg interrupted any rejoinder from Jared, and she rushed to the window and screamed at the mourning doves, who rose in pairs to a higher part of the building.

But Peg's outcries were brought to a halt by something she saw on the pavement below. A long procession of limousines was coming to a halt at her very door. Horns blew, drowning out any cry of doves, men in top hats emerged from the cavernous black vehicles. Police whistles sounded everywhere, like some strident overture.

Jared, unaware of what was transpiring below, was giving one of his own set speeches (he resembled Mr. Hennings in his fondness for long harangues) about how if Mr. Hennings did not return from jail he would close his underground theater and go to London where they had indicated he would be right for a recently discovered fragment of a Christopher Marlowe play.

"Jared, my love, will you come away from the footlights for a moment and tell me if what I am seeing below is actual fact!" Reluctantly, Jared stopped speaking and went to the window.

"For cripes sake!" was all he could get out.

"It must be the Mayor or the Governor, or who knows, the White House!" Peg went on, gaping and screwing up her eyes, for she had mislaid her glasses.

Lifting his top hat to them, for he had caught a glimpse of Peg looking down, was Edward Hennings, free from manacles, and holding more tightly than ever to Estrellita, who was wearing a tuxedo and spats. But when Peg Sawbridge flung open the door on Edward and Estrellita, the financier pushed breezily past her with hardly a glance or word, and went directly to the divan on which Desmond was reclining. The glimpse of the young man's strawberry and cream good looks made any words stick in Edward's throat. He could hardly remember in all his years of worship of male beauty, any complexion to compare with Des'.

"This is my masterpiece," Edward Hennings finally managed to say, pointing to Desmond Cantrell, who blushed furiously, only adding to his pulchritude. "If I had never accomplished another thing in my life, this would have made living worthwhile." He bent down and pressed his lips to Desmond's eyes. Then, pulling out from his jacket pocket the handcuffs the police had used for his arrest, he threw the cuffs to Jared, who caught them as easily as a baseball pro.

"And what are those stains of moisture on your cheeks?" Mr. Hennings addressed the Thespian, "old Hard-Boiled Harder than Nails as Peg calls you."

In reply, Jared buried his face in Mr. Hennings' Palm Beach suit, and the old man was silent until the Thespian got hold of his emotions.

"And I don't suppose you are going to explain where and why you have been all this while," Peg began at last. Her feelings were terribly hurt that Edward was paying no attention to her.

"A case of mistaken identity," Edward was evasive and kissed her repeatedly now, and pulling up her emerald necklace he pushed her lips close with the gems, and then laid two fingers on his own lips, significantly.

"You love to keep everything secret, Edward, my dear. But must mystery always be so thick as it is in your case?"

At this moment, Ramon and three other servants entered, bearing trays of food and refreshment. But all at once everyone became silent because from across the room, they could hear the insinuating notes of the Cuban flute. All eyes turned to Estrellita, who was again favoring them with what Edward called, "one of her little concerts".

At the sounds of the flute, Desmond Cantrell rose up from his divan, and Mr. Hennings caught him in his arms, and the two danced about the room together. Then, Edward released Desmond to Jared, and the two close friends danced even more vertiginously, and then Edward cut in and indicated Peg must dance with one or both of the young men. Before they knew it, everyone present had turned Mrs. Sawbridge's vast room into a veritable dance hall, and all in the room were choosing partners and dancing to Estrellita's music. Even Ramon and the other servant put down their trays, and there was no one who did not choose a partner, until you would have thought you were indeed at some timeless ceremony in honor of Terpsichore.

20

"How dare I criticize him when he has been, after all, my life!"

Peg was speaking to her daughter, Cleo, in the seldom-used side parlor from whose creamy walls hung priceless Impressionist paintings. The unexpected return of Edward and Estrellita, and the subsequent flute and dance entertainment was only hours ago, but that event already seemed to belong to a distant past.

"You evidently think no one else in your long life has done anything for you," Cleo moved closer to her mother.

"Thank you for the *long*, dearest, and remember it dates you also. Old mother, old daughter."

Cleo pulled at her beaded gown, and began to sputter out another diatribe.

"Can't you forbear for a while, Cleo, sweet?" Peg advanced fearlessly to within a few inches of her daughter. "Don't you know, for all our quarrels and disputes and slammed doors and broken crockery you are dearer than life itself to me. And you are, after all, whether you like it nor not, my own flesh and bone, and blood, and heart! Whereas Mr. Hennings...."

"He is even more to you! Why not say it! I know. Without him you would shrivel up like the skeletons of cicadas that are crawling about everywhere in his bedroom."

"That is his laboratory, Cleo, love."

"What on earth do you mean by allowing him to entice those loathsome insects into our home?" Cleo made reference to Mr. Hennings' recent strategem of beguiling the cicadas who sang in one of the hundred-year-old gingko trees to enter one of his principal *salas* (he used the Spanish word for "room" now, almost always.)

"Ah, I was just as disgusted as you, pretty, by the flying things." Peg tried to calm her daughter, whom she feared perhaps more than any other human being, and whose temper was similar to her late husband's in acrimony and pitilessness.

"He is extracting some chemical from the bodies of the male cicadas," Peg tried to explain Mr. Hennings' new avocation. "They are the songsters, you know. The female cicadas are silent."

"All females are silent and invisible where Mr. Hennings is concerned. He despises the sex at heart." And Cleo waited for her mother's rejoinder.

"There I must differ with you again, Cleo, precious. Had it not been for Mr. Hennings!" And she threw up her arms, unable even to imagine what her life would have been had she not known him.

"Ah, yes, I know, you would be a retired whore on the South Side of Chicago today."

"Sweetheart, you are not far from the truth," Peg choked out the words and then hurled this thunderbolt: "I have just learned I have run through everything I own. And the rosiest thing in our future is bankruptcy."

"Mother, please be serious!"

But Peg swept on with, "Can I help it, do you suppose, if he is an entymologist and extracts chemicals from the abdomen of the male cicada? Who knows? Perhaps in those very abdomens he will find the true cure for the Pest."

Cogitating on bankruptcy, Cleo veered off to another topic:

"Mother, if you ask me, I think Des Cantrell looks worse today than when he was dying of the Plague."

"Cleo, you are hard. God, are you ever!"

103

"But you complained father was weak, mother. You've drilled me since birth in never being that!"

"Hard, hard," Peg snivelled on. "I think, my dear, if you will excuse me I'll go into the room now with the cicadas, and try to convey your displeasure to the gentleman who is keeping a roof over our heads at this moment. You and I may yet have to join the cicadas in the boughs of the gingko trees. As I say, my dearest," and here Peg rose and stared at her daughter's shimmering gown, "I believe I will go encourage Edward Hennings in extracting juice from the abdomen of the male cicada. If you ever grow up, you will think back possibly on what a spoiled snot you were when it came to being grateful to the one person who has provided bread for your caustic mouth and the silk and beads to gown your svelte body! And the countless imported cushions for your endless hours in bed!"

It was Cleo's turn now to burst into a crying jag.

"Weep, my darling, do weep! It will clear up your acne perhaps since you cannot resist ladyfingers soaked in rum and whipped cream. Weep on, there's a good girl. Your mother will be in the cicada room if anyone calls."

"Mother, mother, don't leave me when you've crushed me like this. Why, oh why didn't you tell me you were facing bankruptcy? I would have listened."

Peg studied her daughter's eyes briefly. Then:

"Remember, I will be in the cicada room."

Peg blew kisses to the distrait Cleo, and then slammed the door behind her as she exited so that the Impressionist paintings shivered on their long fastenings.

21

"Our chief character flaw, sweet Jared, is we are never satisfied!"

Jared and Peg were seated in what Mrs. Sawbridge called, or miscalled, the Clerestory Room, owing to the many small windows carved out of the ceiling. Miserable Jared was toying with one of the discarded carapaces of the cicadas.

"Oh, your epigrams, Peg. They do me in." He brought the insect carapace briefly to his lips.

"The feeling keeps coming over me like a big black wave, Peg. That our Desmond Cantrell is still somewhere on the shore where the ferryman took him. His soul, I mean. They've returned his body to us, thanks to Edward Hennings, like this cicada shell, but the Desmond I loved so desperately is still somewhere by the black river."

Peg gave one of her cavernous sighs, but at an angry look from her interlocutor, she stemmed back any tears, and, following his example, she picked up a loose cicada shell from the ingrain carpet.

"Desmond will return to his old sweet self, my darling. Mark my words. Don't answer me back now!" She raised her right arm as she had in court room dramas. "Des was so ill, you know that. But he did recover, thanks to Edward. Yes, thank God for Edward. And Desmond's soul is still with him, Jared, and he will be everything he was when he gets stronger.

You see if I am not right. His soul is not by some dark river of the other shore. I know, I know."

"Women are such optimists, such incurable honeysuckers." But Jared did not speak with his old sour conviction. "I will love Des, Peg, even if he is like our cicadas here, just a shell."

"And Jared, listen. Des is even more handsome than when he went away from us."

"I've noticed," Jared's lips moved in a faint smirk and then he laughed.

"Mother, mother.... What kind of a menage are you running now!" Cleo had broken in upon Jared and Peg to utter these words. "Have you seen the condition of the room you've assigned to Desmond? Which was, you might possibly remember, Father's room. I ask you, Mother! Perhaps though, I should go to a hotel to live, for you have turned Father's house into a menagerie."

Mrs. Sawbridge and Jared followed Cleo to Des' room.

"Ah, well, Cleo, I was aware of this. Be calm, won't you, please?"

Peg, however, employed one of her habitual signals of distress, clutching her emerald necklace to her lips as she stared at the "condition" of Father's room.

"Surrounded on all sides by birds!" Thus Cleo described the appearance of the walls, ceilings and floor of Desmond's assigned room.

Taken aback at the ruin around her, Peg managed to get out: "They're only young chimney swifts or swallows, Cleo, love. They've come down unbidden what you would call, I presume, Father's chimney. I hardly think our Desmond would invite them for company."

Desmond looked up from the four-poster bed he was stretched out on, and beamed at the delegation which had burst in upon him. Des looked years younger, and his general seraphic countenance worked on Mrs. Sawbridge, as she later reported, like a constellation of sunbeams. The small, immature swallows nestled against the convalescent boy, one on his head, others on his shoulders, and two or three on his pearl-white naked feet.

Somehow, as the two would later confide in one another, the sight of the swallows moved both Jared and Peg to some strange, intense and uncontrollable emotion so that they almost welcomed Cleo's spiteful anger as a bracer.

But then, at an additional reference to her father on the part of Cleo, something snapped in Mrs. Sawbridge.

"A word with you in my private study!" Peg heard her own words as if they emanated from a recording machine.

"You shall say what you have to say before everyone, Mother, here and now. We needn't mind the birds, after all, and Des and Jared have learned all there is to learn from you, besides, about our personal lives. No, I shan't go to your private chamber even for tea."

"Very well, my dear," Cleo's mother spoke in a silken, almost inaudible voice. "If you do not desire privacy, certainly I do not crave it either. What you will hear, however, may not appease or becalm that spiteful disposition of yours, be advised."

Peg's bosom rose and fell as it did when she played in one of the last-century melodramas selected by – perhaps written by – Jared Wakeman. And, as if on cue, Jared himself now stepped forward like the leading man who will give rapt attention to Peg's stellar speech of incrimination and revelation.

"The man you always refer to as Father, the late Mr. Sawbridge, as if he was the Great Father over all, never was able to earn enough money to feed one of these swallows! Every red cent that went into my palace, as you used to call our home, came from my ingenuity, ceaseless striving and indefatigable efforts to provide you with every convenience, need and luxury."

"That will do, Mother," Cleo cried, but with a note of faltering.

Stepping quickly forward, Peg slapped her daughter across the mouth. Holding her breath as she was accustomed to do when crossed as a small girl, Cleo pretended asphyxiation. Another, heavier blow from her mother restored normal breathing and a kind of calm attentiveness came over the

107

daughter, much as Mrs. Sawbridge had calmed unruly and noisy audiences by merely looking thunderbolts at them.

"Oh, Mother, Mother," Cleo managed faintly to whimper.

"As I say, your adored *Father* could not have had the get-up-and-get or manhood to feed one of these tiny chimney swifts, let alone support a wife and family."

As she said this, Mrs. Sawbridge astonished even Jared by seizing one of the unwary little birds and brought it to her mouth. Then, holding the mesmerized swift with her stage grandeur, Mrs. Sawbridge was about to continue her revelations concerning her late husband when her field of vision took in Desmond, watching her with such admiring awe that Peg burst into choked guffaws. Guffaws which awakened the ire again of her daughter, who now advanced upon her mother, and tore off her emerald necklace and threw it to the floor.

Peg was grateful for this new act of disrespect and hoydenism. She went on: "Over the many years, in which I have provided you with countless beds of roses, I've never heard one 'thank you' from your pouting lips. Whatever my sacrifices for you, the only refrain I've ever heard is 'Father, Father'."

"You have lost the last vestige of any reason in your tired old brain," Cleo tried to fend off the coming revelation.

Jared had sat down on the hardwood floor, entranced by the cream of this melodrama, and was taking mental notes for use in his next production. Then, as the revelation gave evidence it was about to come out, Cleo warned, "I will kill myself!"

The swallows now began rushing through the room, either alarmed or perhaps merely stimulated by this fracas, for swallows accustomed to fly as much as a thousand miles a day, chafe under imprisonment in old houses and empty chimneys.

Looking down at the Thespian, Cleo beseeched: "Go in the next room, Jared, why don't you, and bring out Father's shotgun and let Mother shoot me. Then you'll also be sure of getting even more money from the estate."

Desmond had opened the largest of the windows, and everybody looked up as the swallows, in a rush that their stage manager would have appreciated, flew in almost single file out from the room, into the polluted air of the city.

"All right, all right, old girl," Cleo braved her mother, bemused by the flight of the birds. "Who, then, since you're so prescient, is my father?"

A bit frightened by Cleo's trembling so violently from head to foot, Peg spoke with a bit less rancor, "I think you know, my sweet, the answer to that question, despite your Eastern education, which makes every American girl a bona fide idiot. Why need I say more?" She turned away.

Grasping Peg by the sleeve, Cleo proceeded, "If you tell me my father is that tatterdemalian original inhabitant of Sodom, I will indeed do away with myself."

Peg pulled her sleeve away from Cleo's grasp.

"I will say no more, Cleo, and will let you draw your own conclusions." As in final rehearsals and opening nights, Mrs. Sawbridge was growing very tired, even sleepy. She needed a king-sized cup of Cuban coffee.

Against even her own sense of decorum and taste, Cleo had thrown herself at her mother's feet, as Jared and Des exchanged looks both of relish and unbelief. "Tell me lies, then, Mother. Just tell me the lies you have told me from babyhood, that the man I thought was my father, your Mr. Sawbridge, is in point of fact my real father."

"I will do no such thing. Your father is, was, and always will be the horror of your trundle bed and nursery, Mr. Edward Hennings. Your sisters all had different fathers. But, as my eldest, you were in point of fact sired by the man you loathe, despise and feel only permanent disgust at the sight of. And besides, you look like him. You're very dark for a daughter of mine."

Like some popular Pontiff of the hour Cleo appeared to be

mistaking the hardwood floor for the earth of some welcoming foreign airport, and pressed her lips assiduously to the wood.

"Mother, you have killed me."

"Now, now, darling," Peg chided, and attempted to pull her daughter up from the floor. "What does it matter who sired you, if I love you? What good after all, were men to women like us?" Looking sideways at Des and Jared, she added, "Young men, well, that's perhaps a different story. But you and I, child, have something no man can give or take from us. Get up now, my child. If I love you, the world can turn to ashes."

Cleo rose brokenly like some aged beldame, and as she painfully made her way to her mother's embrace, a few mature swallows flew back into the room, and after a dizzying reconnoitering of ceiling and walls, exited with piercing cries.

22

It wasn't light yet, that's all Des Cantrell remembered later on. Not light and not quite pitch dark. He heard from outside the bats returning from their forays, though sometimes their cries were similar to the chimney swifts'.

Then Des felt the kisses, so hot they resembled cold blades.

Estrellita was bending over him, holding him by the nape of his neck.

"I suppose you think you belong to him now also," Estrellita spoke after a while, and her English had no accent.

"I suppose so," Des mumbled, accepting her burning dry kisses as if he had partaken of them many times before.

"Shall we be slaves together, then?" Estrellita went on, and then, yawning hugely, she lay down beside Desmond Cantrell.

"You mean by him, I suppose, your husband," Desmond managed to free his mouth from hers long enough to say this.

"Who else?" Estrellita muttered, placing her hand on his breast. Des looked about suspiciously, wildly.

"Your lover, Jared, is in bed with Mr. Hennings," Estrellita answered Des' searching expression. Then, at Desmond's registering of utter bereftness, she went on, "But you knew, didn't you, that if he cured you, Jared would have to belong to him? After all, that was the one thing Jared wanted, to have you cured."

"In bed with a scarecrow," Des spoke as if alone.

111

After kissing his breast again and again, Estrellita also now spoke as if she also was alone: "It's too late now for jealousy or envy. I would be glad to exchange my slavery with Edward Hennings for my old slavery in Havana. But see how calm I am, Desmond? The die has been cast. For I exchanged slavery in jail in Havana for slavery in luxury with Edward Hennings. I see now I prefer Cuban slavery, but the Cubans regard me as unfit even for their jails. Tainted meat, they call me. And I've grown used to extravagance and waste. I'm tainted all right, to the bone. Des, let me taste your lips again. Closer, closer. You are the blondest fellow I have ever seen. No angel ever shone so white. Your hair is almost like hay, but your eyelashes are coal black. And your eyes! Do you know I once overheard Jared say to Mrs. Sawbridge, 'Des' eyes are the color of thrush eggs'."

Des began sobbing, dry little convulsive sobs, and Estrellita, taking advantage of his weakness, was removing, piece by piece, all his clothing. She paused a long time over his feet. Calloused though they were (Des was an inveterate jogger) she found them with their high arches and active digits beyond any beauty she had anticipated, and she was busy kissing each of his toes, pausing a long time over his big toe, which she gradually took completely into her mouth.

"I should have died, I guess, after all," Des whimpered. He raised up then to look into her eyes.

"Do you know, Estrellita," he said, "it was all so vivid in the other world. I spoke with some of the Twelve Disciples, Andrew, James, John, especially."

"And Judas and Doubting Thomas?"

But Estrellita had all but knocked the breath out of him, preventing any future speech, by laying her head heavily across his belly and then his groin. Occasionally, in the midst of her exertions and Des' groans of frenzied enjoyment, she would come up like a diver from deep water, and say "I deserve you, Des, for all I've gone through".

Then, extending her naked right arm she silently pointed out what she later explained were brand marks, and then showing her back with the imprint of notched bullhide.

Then again like a deep sea diver, she took a breath and fastened herself far down on the struggling Des Cantrell, causing him to give out one muffled cry after another, while his lips formed foam like the seatide against the beach.

23

"We have a rival!"

Peg Sawbridge had lowered all the lights in her front parlor except for a few little lamps which rested on the floor by the lion claws of a davenport which had been remodelled so many times the whole article resembled a stuffed animal of obscure origin. She addressed her words to Jared who lay with his head in her lap. He snorted.

"Don't believe me, then. Go on. Scoff. It is, after all, your long suit."

"A rival in what category then?"

She kissed him several times before replying:

"Our contender is Jonas Hakluyt."

There was a perfect silence. More than Peg had ever dreamed, the name "Jonas Hakluyt" had struck hard.

Raising up on one elbow, Jared fixed her with a deadly stare: "How could Edward Hennings even meet such a mountebank, let alone take him into his circle...."

"I suppose on one of his endless jaunts through the parks and avenues, seated in his horse-drawn carriage like some deposed member of royalty. Searching, searching, that's Edward."

"Well, don't let him hear you call him deposed, or you might have to go to the poor house after all.... But surely, Peg, Mr. Hennings could not possibly prefer Jonas Hakluyt to either of us!"

He got up now, and gazed down at her.

"Estrellita told Desmond that Edward had confessed he was – at least temporarily – hopelessly taken with Jonas Hakluyt."

"The mastodon falling in love with a harvest mouse!"

They both fell silent. Jonas Hakluyt was, at that particular hour, the rage of the dispossessed young. Though he preached Jesus Crucified and Life Everlasting, it was his raw energy and Herculean proportions (combined with a face of incalculable beauty and russet hair which fell to his thighs) which perhaps was the secret of his being idolized. He refused all offers from the government and the media, and continued to be little else than a street preacher, but his followers increased in numbers daily, and to such an extent that the authorities felt obliged to arrest the young Evangelist almost as many times as he preached the Gospel.

"The detail which finally captivated poor Edward, so says Estrellita, is Jonas' involuntary hemorrhaging from his lips when he is at the height of his oratory."

Jared shrank into himself. Far more perhaps than Peg he felt the danger of a rival in the Young Evangelist. For, say, if Jonas were to become Edward's all-in-all, what chance had *he* and his Theater of Totality?

"But," Jared's face broke into sudden illumination, "consider this, Peg. Jonas Hakluyt is too mad to allow himself to be controlled or netted by one man, when one considers that the man in question is crowding a hundred...."

"I'm afraid Jonas has already been netted, Jared." Peg spoke with that kind of superior knowledge which always irked him. "But the net, sweetheart, is not Mr. Hennings but Estrellita Fuentes."

Jared dropped the palm-straw fan with which he had been violently fanning himself. He stared at the fan as if it were a piece of explanation for what he had heard.

Going directly up to Jared, Peg handed him her own fan.

"Jonas Hakluyt," she spoke as loudly as if she were at the other end of the room, "do you hear me? Jonas Hakluyt, the Young Evangelist, could barely finish his last chautauqua harangue owing to the fact Estrellita had all at once sat down in the front row on a camp stool with both breasts practically bare.... At the sight of her globes, Jonas was too flabbergasted even to bite his lips for his evening hemorrhage."

Jared covered his eyes with Peg's fan, and kept shaking his head.

"And," Peg went on, "the moment Edward (who was seated next to his wife) saw what made the Evangelist tick, our benefactor rose, interrupting the camp meeting, brought Estrellita to the stage and thence on to the pulpit, and while Jonas' eyes struggled like a catch of fish on a hook at the sight of that undraped bosom, Mr. Hennings himself took over the revival audience, telling the auditors the Evangelist was taken ill, and then with total shamelessness, Edward roused the congregation into a mass singing of 'Come to the Church in the Wildwood'." And, as the thousands of young throats sang out the old hymn, Estrellita had persuaded Jonas to sit down beside her, and was soon holding his brawny hands calloused by labor in a lumberjack camp and in various jails throughout the U.S. and Canada. Jonas hemorrhaged then copiously, and Estrellita wiped his mouth and chin dry with her Swiss linen handkerchief. A few minutes later, they drove off, all three in Edward's special carriage. John the Baptist had slipped, had fallen, speared, skewered.

Like Estrellita, Jonas Hakluyt feared, above all, of being taken, captured, held. Yet, like certain wild animals who have experienced captivity for a while, this untamed young man occasionally felt the urge to be captured. He missed his various jails and prisons and straitjackets. He missed also the sometime brief slavery he endured in the homes of young millionaires of either sex. His only feeling of freedom had come to him when Jesus appeared to him one night as he lay in the back room of an orgy parlor, surrounded by naked men who ceaselessly pointed out to one another his incredible endowment, his unspeakable pulchritude. Jonas had risen finally with their effluvia still covering his torso, and made his way down to the river and baptized himself in the name of the Crucified Lord.

But of late his vital energy had been running low, and though his followers were unaware of any diminution of his power and magnetism, when Jonas caught sight of Estrellita and Edward, an iron gong sounded in his painfully constricted temples. He had seen his new, perhaps his final captivity, and his new, permanent jail door had opened to receive him.

Jonas was also aware that Estrellita's beauty was only the mask for his real captor and lover, Edward Hennings. In fact, after having lain naked with Estrellita a few hours, he had gone unbidden into Edward Hennings' private sleeping chamber, and had sat down on a stool by the Master. Edward Hennings was not asleep. In fact, people said he never slept, and when, on those rare occasions he felt the need of slumber, he merely swallowed the petals of one of his jungle flowers, and was again as alert as a hawk in flight.

Jonas stared at his enslaver, and kept wiping away the perspiration that gathered on his forehead and descended to his perforated lips. "I will never renounce Him," Jonas spoke, after an interminable wait (it seemed more like days passing). "Never, never. I will die first."

"Who asked you to renounce anybody, fool?" Edward broke the timeless silence. "Don't you blaspheme, however, by even suggesting the possibility of your betraying Him?"

"No, no!" Jonas rose from the stool and made a queer threatening gesture at his kidnapper.

"You are free to go," Edward spoke in his silky, nearly inaudible centenarian voice. "You may take Estrellita with you if you desire."

Jonas Hakluyt sat down on the stool again, and great, dry, almost silent sobs rose out from his rib cage.

"Take off your shirt, will you, and sob like that, Jonas. I want to study how the bones of your chest got put together."

A fierce oath began to form itself on the Evangelist's lips, but when the oath died within his throat, his fingers began dreamily unbuttoning his shirt. When the garment fell from him, he obeyed again and sobbed in a perfunctory but perhaps even more dramatic manner. The bones of his ribs stood out, and moved like some fantastic accordion under the searching pupils of old Edward Hennings.

"You have two navels. Are you aware of that?" Mr. Hennings observed, and then wrote something in one of his innumerable calf-skin notebooks.

Jonas kept looking down at himself, and then began putting on his shirt with clumsy, heavy fumblings.

"All the doors of this establishment are wide open, Jonas, so don't stand there like you were in chains. You may leave now with Jesus, or you may stay here with me."

Jonas could not restrain a convulsive attack of groans and dry sobs as he heard the new blasphemy. He raised his fists, he cursed Edward, cursed then his whole life, damned his parents and then, in the midst of his rage and grief, he did what had always been required of him in the various jails and prisons where he had starred. He stripped quietly and stood at attention before his new and final captor and judge.

"Free to go, I said." Mr. Hennings had never been so flint-hard, pitiless. But the view of Jonas entirely bare as he had come into the world caused a slight constriction in the old financier's throat. He coughed spasmodically.

Sprayed by the effluvia of Mr. Hennings' paroxysm, Jonas knelt down languidly by the bed where the new jailer lay coughing. "I said every door is open to you, so you need not fear you have deserted Him." Ancient, older than the hills, Edward Hennings spoke with his eyes on the ceiling. "Yes, Jonas, yes, I see He is at your side even now as you sputter and fume." Jonas silently extended his lips to his persecutor. Mr. Hennings began kissing his new disciple. The sweat which had been accumulating under the thick black hair of Jonas Hakluyt all at once descended over the young Evangelist's brow, then to blind his eyes with its salty sting and from thence in one enveloping sheet, the water spattered over the ancient man's lips, as the two remained clasped one to the other like drowning sailors. Outside, the light now appeared cold, like November, when it was, as the cicadas' song kept announcing, tropical July.

24

The moral ruin of Peg Sawbridge came about in this way. The process-servers and the repossession agents of her $40 million enclave were already at the gates, to use her phraseology, for Edward Hennings had told her as often as the clock moved its minute hand that unless she signed a certain paper, he could not save her. "And you will join the homeless and the derelicts for whom you have shed so many tears, though you deposited so few coins in the poor box for them," he reminded her. The process-servers and repossession agents had arrived a few hours after Peg and Edward Hennings had had an argument of such bitterness that even the hard exterior of Jared Wakeman was shattered, and he broke down, unequal to the pain of witnessing such a deadly duel between his two most important patrons.

Peg had defended what Edward called her milk-and-water liberalism to which she had only given, after all, lip service, and she had chided him for carrying banners proclaiming the worthlessness of the human race, and dismissing as fiftieth-rate American civilization with its shoddy propaganda of freedom while enslaving mankind by reason of its monopoly of wealth, bombs and painted dreams (his Bolshevism).

But what had always cut Mrs. Sawbridge to the quick was Edward's low opinion of women, even though he had always made partial exception in her case.

But when exhausted by their fray, Peg saw that she was without doubt going to be put into the street, homeless, penniless, and with Edward as an implacable foe instead of performing his role as her lifelong protector and friend, she gave up any shred of pride or vanity and went to his study (he now, of course, as she suspected, owned all that had been hers).

Mrs. Sawbridge, with the morning breeze moving her white muslin gown, told Mr. Hennings she was ready to abdicate if he would allow her to stay on in her fifty-room conclave. It was odd, she noticed, since he was a foe of nicotine (one of the instruments by which the U.S. enslaved the rest of mankind), he was smoking with intense, concentrated pleasure a Havana puro. But then, she supposed, he smoked it because it was not American.

Peg scanned for hours on end the long legal document Mr. Hennings demanded she sign. Famous names of attorneys graced the top of the bond paper of so stiff a quality that one risked cutting the fingers of one's hand to the bone when touching it. Peg had never scanned such a collection of infamous statements. *Mein Kampf* would seem an amiable and constructive document by comparison. And she was to sign such a collection of statements in violation of all she believed?

But the thought of homelessness! The idea of never wearing jewels again, or having Ramon bring her a ladyfinger filled with almond-flavored whipped cream! And what would Cleo do as a homeless girl? Die in the shelters with bedbugs, scabies and incurable syphilis and finally the Pest itself, which would perhaps mercifully close her eyes?

Peg barely read the heresies, barely saw she was signing away her soul with such dicta as:

> The entire women's movement would graft on the Constitution the clitoris for its Great Seal of the U.S., and men, as eunuchs, would be demoted to Third Class Citizens.
>
> ....

Freedom, after all, can be guaranteed only to those who are unfit for life itself.

....

All races are inherently created to enslave all other races for the simple reason the human race is the uncurable plasma of the Pest itself, and the Pest is the final perfect form of the total failure of humanity.

....

The American mind, if one can flatter it by saying it has one, this same mindless America, depraved by incurable addiction to the products of the Merchants who control the very diastole and systole of their helpless customers, long, even pant for a Nero for president.

The lunatic horror of what Peg Sawbridge perused and was expected to sign her name to in approval was doubly unnerving for her partly because she suspected that, in all its deranged rhetoric, there lurked some shred of truth. Yet, truth or lies, she could not refuse to sign and take the alternative: walk out of her mansions now and die on the street, or remain a traitor and apostate but backed by luxury, comfort, dozing security. So she signed her name in large, bold letters that belied her age, her incipient arthritis, her irregular heart beat, and her years of aristocratic prostitution and high-handed real estate deals.

Mr. Hennings, grinning, read over his own document, stared at Peg's signature (he called it her autograph), then kissed her on each of her digits and kneaded her bosom insincerely, and then, to make her disgrace official, placed a diamond necklace on her still lovely, rose throat.

After her abdication, Mrs. Sawbridge looked out the window and saw the process-servers and the other officials from the Real Estate Olympus driving away in their inky black limousines through whose windows one could glimpse only what looked like a soot-storm.

Peg walked to the middle of her ingrain carpet and rang a brass-coloured bell she had once cajoled away from a young man in the Salvation Army. She had also pinched his kettle at the same time, and before driving off in a cab, had handed him her address. When he called for both kettle and bell, she agreed to restore the articles only if he would allow her to admire, without interruption, his farm-boy, stalwart physique, for they both, she pointed out, had common prairie farm origins. She remembered all the details of her sin now she had stooped to lower herself to the point in which she yielded to an old Bolshevik into signing a virtual abdication from her sex and the human race to boot.

"All our presidents, Ramon," she quoted from her own document, "all, when not outright imbeciles, were rotters to the core." She spoke first in English, then in her own brand of Castillian Spanish. "Rotters, Ramoncito, *cabrones*, to the ninth degree." Then she broke down and boo-hooed.

To Peg's inconsolable distress she found that Jared, who had been able to snitch a copy of her surrender-document, found her apostasy and blasphemies to which she had affixed her signature "hilariously funny".

"Hilarious?" Peg shouted at him, as Ramon held the oversized spoon of whipped cream to her rougeless lips. "You dare brazen me in my own house and tell me my sacrilege and treason are a joke?"

"Peg darling," Jared tried to subside from guffawing, "you seem to have that middle-class high-minded imbecility Edward points out in the New York book reviewers whose columns he once enjoyed wiping on the rectums of female rhinoceroses. And note, as you will, of course, he chose the female of the species."

Taking in breath after breath, her pupils distending, then narrowing, Peg Sawbridge made sounds like water coming from a pump being primed with difficulty, then she made sounds that resembled the death rattle, but the fact was Peg Sawbridge was beginning to laugh. Little choking laughs at first, then great, mammoth cascades. She laughed until she was purple in the face, laughed until she was pale, laughed until, to her shame, she wet her panties.

"You men are so lucky with your water-works," she reverted to the epoch of her Montana youth. "You can hold your water so much more easily than we poor gals."

Ramon came in with fresh under-things, and helped her to change behind a dressing room screen. They heard her laughter louder than ever behind her cover. "And, Jared, sweetheart, after all, my home is saved! I have perjured myself, but my home is mine! We can go on with our Theater, love, and with our lives!"

Peg Sawbridge alternated now between ecstatic happiness she was a free woman, and indignation and ire that it was Edward Hennings who was the actual proprietor of her "many mansions".

"I am about as much mistress here as the scrubwoman who comes on Thursdays."

"She comes on Tuesdays," Cleo reminded her mother as she was passing through the parlor.

Jared took a seat nearer than usual to Peg – he had chosen the recently upholstered green silk throne chair once used by Peg's last husband. The feel of the silk always made him feel more tolerant of life, including even Peg.

"I wish you would renounce the nicotine habit," Peg vented her ill temper on Wakeman, lost in a cloud of blue-white smoke. "True, you don't use the drugs which have, Edward says, made America a nation of meringue brains."

"Excuse me, Peg, but have you looked out the window recently?" Jared changed the subject and blew a long thread of smoke towards the ceiling.

"Of all professions, Jared, it is the actor who should eschew nicotine. Your voice is getting so hoarse and muffled, and opaqué!"

"Peg, you haven't answered my question," Jared pursued, but stamped out his cigarette. "They are still out there. Now, now, don't whine. I don't mean the process-servers, either."

Leaping up, Peg went to the window, and after gazing, threw her head back in frenzied displeasure and incredulity.

Her diamond earrings swung violently against her cheeks. "Who are those horrible young riffraff standing out there against my entrance-way, Jared? Why, there must be a hundred of them! No! More!"

"Can't you read their signs and banners?"

"I broke my glasses," Peg blubbered.

"You were too proud and beautiful ever to wear them."

Peg sat down on Jared's lap like old times and smoothed his eyebrows.

"The banners and signs say, Peg, 'What are you doing, Jonas, in the house of Jezebel and the Witch of Endor'. Another banner reads 'Jonas, unless you come back to us we will come up there to claim you'."

Peg rose up from Jared's lap and rushed to the window. She flung it open, though usually she called on Ramon to perform this strenuous feat. Cupping her hands, she called down to the crowd of boys and young women assembled below: "Have you no homes of your own? Go back to where you came from! Aren't you grateful the city is keeping you in shelters and feeding you in soup kitchens? Why, then, do you invade the premises of a woman who has kept her own shoulder to the wheel these many years, and who never accepted a penny of public charity? Learn to labor and to wait, and you'll have no energy for street violence!"

Cries of unrestrained, frothy rage answered her. The sound reminded Jared of cataracts of water in a storm on the lake. Reminded him still more of isolated, distant wild beasts. He shrugged his shoulders, found an old bottle of V.S.O.P. brandy and put just a few drops on his tongue, and a dash more on his temples.

A rock came crashing through the window.

Peg moaned rhythmically and Jared recognized in her outcry the intense pleasure she was receiving from all the tumult below.

"By the way," Jared addressed Peg, who had stretched herself out on the ottoman, "your Young Messiah is coming down the hall."

At that moment, just as in their own private theatricals, Jonas Hakluyt crossed the threshold. He wore a kimono of extreme costliness and age from which hung here and there frayed, refulgent gilt tassels.

"I think we're seeing the end of Peg's rule. She acts like the last Tsarina in some 1918 movie." Des was sitting bolt upright, dressed to the nines, healthy and brash and listening brightly like in old times to Jared. And why shouldn't Des listen so rapt to Jared, who was, after all, the only one he had ever loved, and in whom the sun rose and set, and where the ground Jared walked on would ever be covered with kisses – Des!

"She is like any of those doomed queens all of a sudden," Des offered a concurring opinion. "But why is her rule at an end just now? I thought Mr. Hennings had renewed her lease on all these lofts."

"I think that was all sleight of hand. As a matter of fact, I think Mr. Edward Hennings himself may be in financial trouble. But then, he loses ten or twelve fortunes every year and gets them all back again another year. But while you were so sick, Des, and don't pout like that and pretend you weren't, while you were *away*, then, if that sounds better, Des, Edward Hennings took in this new Messiah; some cowhand from the West, who has a huge following of homeless crazies whose average age is fifteen. That's what that mob is doing out there. The police and the city authorities have told Peg she will be in real trouble this time unless she gets rid of Jonas Hakluyt and his crew. So, you see...."

"What are those sounds now?" Des wondered, and moving suddenly, spoiled the press of his Palm Beach trousers.

Jared listened, despite his irritation at having what he was saying interrupted.

"Oh, the music you mean, Des.... She claims she requires music when she is engaged in writing her recollections, not for publication, however, as Mr. Hennings says they would publish used toilet paper today and get the Book of the Week Club to merchandise it if the paper had on it the shit of some noted sex maniac killer or White House crook of the hour. So she hires young down-and-out musicians. Good ones. Great ones. And as they strum or harp or twang she writes down her life from Montana up to now. I've read some of her jottings. They're riveting to the eye, because she doesn't realize how much she is telling.... Yes, listen to that now. It's a zither. Next we'll hear some Caribbean sax or a new ragamuffin who plays the jew's harp or sweet potato. And do you know, she gives them sometimes actual genuine gold coins? She doesn't know the value of anything today. 'Where did you get gold coins?' I queried her, and she answered back, 'Edward told me they're legal tender again, and since he's leasing me (here she choked up) he tossed some right at me, and I stooped to gather them up for my musicians'."

Des stretched out on the floor, perhaps to be closer to Jared's bare feet.

"But the big shebang is coming, Des. Edward Hennings has been closeted incommunicado for days now with Jonas Hakluyt. Priming him. That's the word. 'I'm priming the Messiah,' Mr. Hennings explains. Fact is, though, Jonas primed or sandpaper-dry is going to address his followers from the balcony here. The mob of his followers anyhow has been alerted and they're down there gathering in strength to hear him. For they're in mutiny because he's up here when his place is down there with the rags and smell and the howls."

"Jared," Des began and stood up now to his full height. He spoke in his cured, strong, leading-man's voice, "Jared, shouldn't we leave now? I mean, what do we need a riot for? Why can't we go to our place, Jared? This isn't our home."

Desmond was spared, for the moment, his friend's gathering rage by the entrance of their hostess and their guide.

"That's just the news I needed to hear," she launched into her own attack on them. "Just when I need you, and as Des points out, when there's every evidence down there of a riot, you two clear out."

"Come off it," Jared's anger turned now on Peg instead of Des. "You invited that old mountebank here in the first place with his Cuban bride. You must have known he'd do something to get you up to your eyebrows in mischief. And, oh, do you love mischief, Peg. You dote on riots. What will Des and me staying or not staying add to your peace of mind or your safety?"

"Traitors, traitors, I knew it. Cleo warned me about you, but I wouldn't listen. All right, go. Clear out. Both of you. And don't ever bother to come back, do you hear? There's the back door, where even the police won't see you skidooing."

But the sudden realization Jared might go out of her life and leave her without "ideas" or "roles", without footlights or applause or love (even of the kind Jared could bestow), dried up her threats. She changed tunes. She countermanded. "For God's sake, boys, wait! I'll do anything for you. Don't leave me when things are blowing up all around. You know, don't you, Edward and Estrellita are leaving. As soon, I suppose, as the riot is over."

Peg threw herself into the arms of Jared and Des. They all held one another as strongly and devoutly as if they were members also of some evangelical sect of their own. "You wouldn't want to miss hearing the Messiah give his speech now, after all," Peg broke away from hugs and kisses long enough to quip. And there was a faint snickering and then sighs and groans.

What could they do but stick together, after all?

25

Peg Sawbridge wandered about through her innumerable rooms like the moon itself. "I am Luna," she often soliloquized on her rounds, "I bathe all with my wan light."

The terror was still with her of being dispossessed. Her fear was constantly reinforced when she looked down on the street below and saw the homeless crowd there waiting for "Messiah". The impoverished, driven by millionaire landlords into the streets, and the concurrence of the Mayor and the White House, brought back to vivid immediacy her own early youth and misery before Edward Hennings appeared with his fairy's wand.

Peg, in the dead of night, often burned color photos of the Mayor and the President. There had to be somebody to loathe and fear, hate and despise, and these two spokesmen for the real estate and nuclear empires became easy targets for her anger. She had hated her own father, after all.

Yes, the homeless brought her in her midnight-to-dawn pacing back to the days when Mr. Hennings had found her unshod and flimsily garbed on Michigan Avenue, near the Chicago Art Institute.

"Edward! Edward! He is the architect of my life," she cried, and then blindly opened a door she did not recognize. Directly in the line of her imperfect vision, on a brand new mattress lay the Antinous of the hour, Jonas Hakluyt, until only a few days ago the god only of the young unwashed and unhoused.

He showed a fiercely blackened eye and a badly cut upper right lip. His rather massive sex lay uncoiled like a live water eel.

Luna let flow from her barely opened mouth a kind of melodious but afflicted arpeggio of notes.

He opened his good eye, then closed it against the sight of her. He made no attempt to cover his member, but lay back like the original model for male pulchritude, worshipped from the earliest caves to the ungifted, tacky present. Why should he, after all, cover what so countless many admirers had sung so many praises to?

"It's your followers who keep me awake," Luna gave a lame excuse for her appearance now.

"Liar," he muttered between his horse-like teeth, and spat a little against the embossed wallpaper. His right hand, larger than his left to such a degree it looked almost deformed in its sinewy development, scratched at the hairs around his navel, which winked now like an eye at her.

"Your followers, Jonas, are growing restless. They can't abide your staying here with me. They want speeches from you, not silence under my roof."

"I don't make speeches." He raised up on one elbow and then sleepily, casually looked down at his member as if it were, apart from him, something that had appeared unbidden upon his belly.

"I turn flesh into living flame!" he spoke under his breath.

At a queer look of invitation from him, Luna seated herself by his thigh. As she looked more closely, she saw a whole network of scars and broken veins across his breast and abdomen. "You must get out of here, Jonas, while you still can. My mistake, after my initial meeting the Beast, was I not only stayed under his jurisdiction, but could not give up, not so much his bankrolls, as life without his direction and command. He was always in my thoughts."

Jonas Hakluyt tore at his matted hair, and then, dropping

his hands for a moment, crushed his crimson-streaked mouth against hers. He kissed her with the kind of impatient vigor a half-grown boy attacks a just ripened peach. She made a feeble outcry against the pain, but then pressed her own mouth deeper into his.

Freeing himself all at once from her kisses, he let strings of thick saliva flow out of his mouth to the comforter.

"He operated on me," Jonas said, half complaint, half relief in his bass voice. "A cyst on my loins or over my kidney, to hear him. Anyway, somewhere, he cut into me."

"Operated?" Luna wondered. He pulled her toward him again.

"But then," Jonas started up, and to her wonder he began to cry, but his crying quickly ended in a cough that was like a horse whinnying.

"I felt then all the pain I had ever had from when I was born till now, leaving me, as he cut into me, and yes, his kisses, his kisses as he cut at the growth on my loins or kidneys with the heated steel, for he said his kisses were stronger than any ether against the pain of the knife."

Luna rose and went to the window.

"What are you doing up and away from me!" He sounded as imperious as Edward Hennings. "Get back over here when I am telling you of the most important event in my life!"

Her face was still wet with his kisses as she lay down beside him.

"Then if what you say is so, it's too late for you." She was speaking as she did in insomnia. "His gifts are so enormous, and I speak from the experience of forty years, maybe more, I forget how old I am, for he has given me such lasting youth and appeal, or so I'm told, though my soul tells me I am five thousand years old. He has taken everything from me but a tiny paper-thin slip of memory. Now you have gone down on him also. Cyst, growth, you fool, it was your soul he cut out of you and took for his own."

Jonas Hakluyt bellowed loud enough to emulate the Eumenides fire engines. The walls of the ten-storey building rocked and trembled in every crevice, then settled down as if about to disintegrate into powder to the street below.

"Go down somewhere," he told her, "Go and fetch me a big cup of something steaming and scalding hot. And don't be gone all night or day or whatever the meridian may be. On the double, hear? March!"

Before she went she gave his cut lips a famished touch, touching at the same time his sex in a kind of desperate gathering of strength from that flesh.

26

"So you want to leave, do you, you damned spoiled little snot! After all that's been done for you, little Lord Fauntleroy is not receiving all his lordship feels is his due."

On shouting all this out, Jared Wakeman offered to belt Des one, but then thought better of it.

"After all," Jared proceeded, "I should remind myself that you are rich, and have a Dad and doting Mom to soothe your troubled little brow. But *they* weren't able to cure you of the Pest though, were they?"

"Jared, you know I didn't have the Pest. For Christ's sake, how can you even think such a thing?"

"You not only had the Pest, you ass, but you were dead and all but buried. Your death certificate was signed and processed. Wake up, will you, for once in your life. And now when you're only half well, you want to up and leave. Well, go ahead, get! I'm staying. At least Peg and Edward Hennings are taking care of me."

"Have you looked outside lately, Jared? The whole place is surrounded with Jonas Hakluyt's crazy followers, and for every follower there must be at least five police details. We're all liable to be arrested or murdered. And listening in on a phone conversation Mr. Hennings was making, I found out that your venerated patron is some kind of international con-man and secret agent to boot!"

"All right, who saved your life? Some lily-white little M.D.? You'd be rotting in some Protestant cemetery if it hadn't been for Edward Hennings and Estrellita."

"Let's not get started on her," Des all but gagged as he spoke these words. "I can't believe I am where I am, and I also can't believe such a place as we're in exists."

"Suit yourself, then. Go! Skidoo! See if I care. Go on, take your whey-faced innocent puss out of my sight! I'm sick to death of you. I've wasted years of my life taking care of you, and trying to make you an actor. And then, when you catch the Pest, and even die of it, it's through my efforts you was restored to life for the benefit of your doting millionaire parents. Go on, go out and tell the police detail of our finest what a nice boy you are, and how when your Dad dies, you'll be like him, a multi-millionaire. Go. Scat."

Jared's mouth curled in sour triumph when he saw Des wilt at his speech. Des could no more walk out of the room, walk out of the Sawbridge tier of floors, than he could jump out the window. His knees threatened to buckle as he stood before Jared, and he sat down on the nearest chair and began to whimper.

As Jared snickered, Des managed to get out, "I guess I know when I'm licked".

Jared simmered down a bit in his turn and sat down on the floor at Des' feet.

"You know me better than I do myself, Jared." He reached for Jared's hand. "I could no more leave you than... than...."

"Than what, simpleton?" But Jared spoke with less fury and spite.

"Your love is all I have, Jared."

"Well, don't screw up your eyes when you say it then, like we was at a colored funeral."

"Why can't you ever let me tell you how much I love you?"

"Because I already know it," Jared shot back now. "You never seem to realize how much I love you!"

"Because you never tell me," Des choked out, his face

133

coloring violently.

The screams of the police cars rose then, making further talk useless.

Peg Sawbridge, or Luna, like the moon, never slept at all. She wandered from room to room of her triple-mortgaged mansion, but always came back to the balcony which overlooked the square, now filled with the disciples of Jonas Hakluyt. They were all pathetically young, she conceded, most of them under twenty, all homeless, and most of them in different stages of the Pest. Their leader, rather, their god, appeared from time to time, to encourage them and bless them, but he was, they saw, a prisoner.

It was therefore Luna who made the most effort to encourage and comfort them, in view of Jonas' detention. "In my youth, children," Luna spoke in her swimming unsteady contralto, "and I thank God I was young then and not today, for in my youth, Venus did not confer on her votaries the terrible gift fate has vouchsafed to you."

"Release him, give us Jonas," their voices drowned her out, but without their accustomed tone of anger and menace.

"He will be coming to you, dear ones. We are giving him rest and nourishment after his operation. A case of proud flesh, that's all. Surgery has been resorted to. Cure is in sight. He will return to you.

"I said," Luna continued, "that I was blessed in being young at a time when Eros did not conceal within his firebrands a deadly virus. And the world then had so many avenues, so many windings and turnings."

"Give us Jonas," a young man screamed, stepping out toward the police cordon. "Surrender him to us, you faded whore."

Luna bowed graciously to insults. After all, she had known little else in her life than abuse from husbands, daughters, Jared Wakeman, and the emperor of vilification himself, Edward Hennings. "I love all of you! Love directs my every motion and breath!"

Groans of fettered rage made the whole square tremble as

in the aftershock of an earthquake.

"Can't you see I am love," Luna cried, and she produced now, like some itinerant magician, several gay colored handkerchiefs and waved them like flags to the assembled disciples.

For some reason they were all subsided into silence. They began settling down like children at a matinee, sitting on the grass under the sycamore and locust trees from whence the cicadas sang now, warning Luna that frost was only a few weeks away at most, and before frost came, Edward Hennings, her savior, would be leaving, consigning her to process-servers, and perhaps even the police.

"I know what bereavement means," Luna now held perfect attention from the disciples. "I have lost all my lovers! I am in perpetual widowhood. I say I have lost all my lovers. Except one! But can one call Edward Hennings, children, a lover? I believe in fact he is an immortal. Believe? What am I saying? Know! Yes, know, dear ones. But he has one mortal weakness. He cannot abide cold weather. So when you hear the cicadas and know the cold is on its way, he leaves me, accompanied by his bride, Estrellita, who, for all I know, may be a hundred also, though at times when I hold her to me, I see she cannot be more than fourteen. Then, if her true age is a puzzle, what about her sex? One day, as I clasp her to my breast, she is, I swear, a man, and the next afternoon as she presses against me she is a woman. So *you* feel bereft, my loves, but your bridegroom does not leave you for a change of seasons! He is all seasons in one. But like you, and your leader, dear ones, had I not met Edward on that broad Chicago avenue, I would have had no bearings, no direction. One of you called me a whore. I could not have even been that had Edward Hennings not raised his wand."

Actually, Luna, at this point in her speech, began to snivel, but as if she saw her director, Jared Wakeman, bearing down on her, she checked herself, and her eyes and nose were dry as tinder.

"I would be the last to deny Venus," Luna eloquentised.

"Even today, I run every risk to obey her commands, and those of her divine son. I would risk his arrows in the teeth of...." she stopped then. "Venus, Venus," Peg Sawbridge was incoherent at the thought of the omnipresent, the ubiquitous Pest. Then, collecting herself, she cried, "I was one of you! I am one of you still. I am you!"

Blinded by her tears, choked by her sobs, she felt the hard arm of Jonas Hakluyt pulling her in. Before she could collect herself, he stood where she had harangued his followers a moment before.

At the sight of Jonas, the multitude on the grass rose in unison, and catapulted out his name in a deafening chant.

"I will never forsake you, never, like the army of lovers of this benighted woman!" Here he pointed to Peg Sawbridge beneath his towering height. "But I have been gathering new strength, children, new ammunition, say. Yes, I too, beloved, need rekindling. My fire, even my perpetual flame, languishes at times."

Loathe, despise, hate passionately as he did that congeries of pestilence he called the Great City, still Edward Hennings was the first to point out it contained within its corrupt maw all things, a kaleidoscope of all the horrors, failures and egregious successes of the Beast that has no Name but incalcuable power, and whose final apotheosis is the Pest itself.

To the best of her recollection of the terrible event which followed her bidding adieu to Jonas' followers and disciples, a hand, certainly not hers, bestowed on the Young Messiah a flowing, thin, gossamer garment which he assiduously wrapped about him. But as Jonas did so, not so much the garment itself burst into flames, as the consecrated body under it. Indeed, that garment was the last substance to be kindled and consumed into the most insubstantial of ashes.

His amarinthine head was not consumed, but fell to the street below and was caught by one of his male disciples, who swore later the lips opened and spoke to him.

Even the police, the plainclothes men, the government agents, and countless other representatives of authority were baffled, made mute, and stood in impassive puzzlement.

Mrs. Sawbridge went into convulsions. She was too ill to be hospitalized, but several world famous specialists were summoned. The usual hypodermics were administered.

Cleo, thinking her mother was about to die, about to leave her, required medical assistance, finally, more than Mrs. Sawbridge, who at the last moment, unaccountably revived, and summoned Ramon. Only one thing attested to her incomplete recovery: she kept asking for her "dear, her only one," Jonas. "Where is he, where is my beloved?"

Mr. Hennings was at his most imperious, grand and incontrovertible during the police investigation.

But what was the evidence? What was the garment which had consumed one who after all was wanted by the police in twelve states and Canada for subversion, riot, criminal conspiracy and anarchy.

And the head had, like most of the body, disappeared.

The police went over and over again with Mr. Hennings the allegations that the mob of followers of the anarchists had broken in upon the front staircase of Mrs. Sawbridge bearing the decapitated head of the young Messiah and were only dissuaded from pillage and murder by the presence of Mr. Hennings carrying in his right hand a billiard ball which the crowd of followers mistook for a bomb, and turned tail and fled.

"I knew Emma Goldman well," Mr. Hennings was heard talking to a plainclothes man and a representative of his Honor the Mayor. "She was all lemon water," he told the rapt listeners. "Understood nothing of history. Like all women, the sight of a handsome male caused every idea in her brain to dissolve and float heavenward, while her cheeks flamed with desire, her bosom surged like lava."

The inquest ended here.

It was Jared who had handed the Young Messiah the fatal

garment. No, amend that to this: Jared was handed the garment by Mr. Edward Hennings and Jared, in turn, handed it to the Evangelist. But before the garment bestowal, Jared, like Mrs. Sawbridge, had opened a door by pure chance, and inside, facing him, without a stitch to cover him, was the savior who had turned everyone's head, including of course Jared's own.

"I knew you would know," Jonas addressed the Thespian. "I knew once you had seen me you would know everything."

"Your followers are still out there," Jared spoke these words in order to say something.

"Look at me, though," Jonas advised him. "Take a good, long look."

Jonas' skin, over which countless purple scourges rested, was the color of sun-drenched sand. His eyelashes were sprinkled with a something resembling gold dust. The purple scourges appeared to have mouths, voices also, calling out to Jared.

Jonas' goatsucker voice rose just as the first streaks of the morning touched the extinct craters of the city of canyons.

"I have been waiting for Aurora to show them my affliction," Jonas told the Thespian. "Now I can go out and reveal the full extent of it! In my birthday suit!"

"But you don't need to let them see you like this," Jared protested.

"I want them to love me as I am and was. I know what your face is seeing. Go hide from them. Don't let them know I have it! You are saying leprosy was a sacred affliction compared to this." The preacher's voice rose an octave.

"But what if they want you just as you are."

"Just as I am," Jonas broke into the old hymn song and then, so unlike the chief of apostles, choked out a purely human sob. "My life is at an end."

"What if they find a cure, Jonas?"

"I can't be cured of being only a man. They thought I was proof against the failings of the flesh.

"They thought," he added, putting a hand on Jared's brow, "I was beyond flesh".

The Chuck-Will's-Widow kind of voice now took over completely.

"You'll stand beside me, Jared," the nightjar voice rose higher, and he took Jared's hand in his.

They went out then together, that is how it was, Jared recalled. And on the way, someone handed him the garment.

His followers below, many of whom had not slept in days, caught his golden refulgence. Cries that appeared to come from dirigibles or mountains rose higher, slowly in tempo. Then those cries rose to greater volume, then became piercing, voluminous. Ears everywhere were split, as the confusion and pandemonium took over. The dawn revealed their god a leper, but whereas leprosy in their fingered Bibles had something finally holy (as Jonas warned Jared), their leader's purple patches over his golden skin betokened that God had forsaken or mocked them, betokened treason, betrayal, lies deceit, hypocrisy. Even the cross would not be punishment for a leader who had only the incurable patch of the Pest.

"I am innocent of all charges. I am your god!" Jonas cried.

A giant of a man of dubious race stepped forward below, and cried, "Come down then, or we come up, Jonas Hakluyt."

Then the garment was extended and slowly his arms went into this almost thistle-down cloth of insubstaniality. And then the flames! The consumption by fire burning from blood.

"But they didn't come from the bathrobe or whatever that I gave him was. No! They came from his own blood, flesh and bones! The fire was all from inside and on top of his flesh!"

Granted, Jonas Hakluyt was the supreme experience, in many ways, of all their lives, the consumption, the unforgettable, the experience in which they reached their highest selves, his sudden appearance and departure only in the end left them more like themselves. They had seen the apotheosis, they had touched the palpable presence of what they had always believed in and waited for. Yet when he had departed, they had only what they had been before. He was everything to them and yet nothing. There was their daily life, their daily selves to go on with. The burden of utter banality, shoulders aching under the diurnal care and boredom of life in the Great City.

The cicadas were as silent as the dead preacher. Inside her many rooms, Peg Sawbridge listened in frozen terror to her earthly savior and his spouse, Estrellita, making preparations to depart.

Edward had always left her at the approach of frost, yet this time she knew he would leave her forever. And on his departure her financial ruin was assured! So she braved his privacy, she opened one forbidden door after another and surprised Edward and Estrellita in slithery close embrace. Seeing Peg, he almost pushed his bride from his kisses and came out into the corridor, to take Peg's arm in his.

"I am not leaving you with nothing," Peg heard him begin his explanation of his final desertion, leaving her to face eviction from her tenancy of the grandest of mansions. "A Mr. Niemoyer will place you in an even finer domicile," Edward began.

"Not *the* Mr. Niemoyer, the Prussian!" she heard her own suffocated voice.

She accepted one of his pills and a deep glass of spring water. She barely listened then to his harangue. He told her of his surprise that not only she but Jared and Desmond had been taken in by the young zealot evangelist.

"Violent deaths revive in us," Edward Hennings went on, as he consulted an airlines schedule, "and bring back to us all the past Saviors, Messiahs, Princes of the Impossible, new Nazarenes."

"No, no," Peg heard herself cry and plead. "I will not stay to listen. I will go down and join his followers first!"

"But they have all gone, dear heart. The crowd of followers and the police. The police won't come here anymore. I have settled everything."

But she was only hearing his earlier speech from years and ages past, how Jonas Hakluyt was like Jesus, a young man only comfortable with other young men together with a few fallen women, like herself, who worshipped the ground he walked on, the sweat that dribbled from his armpits and thighs.

"Yes, and tell over and over again now, Edward, how you found me unwashed and unshod, a waif from Montana on the streets of Chicago."

"I think I finally got Jonas to see just before he was immolated that Jesus is an invention of everybody's fancy, and neither divine nor in fact a person. The original Jesus, I told him was probably a Greek or Roman, trained of course in some desert in the healing arts, and who was only comfortable, like Jonas, with young men and an occasional Magdalene. I did not say to him, mind you, that Jesus gave his body to his Twelve Disciples, though at the last supper, that is what he expected them to do, once taken from the cross."

Peg Sawbridge was barely aware she was listening to these hackneyed blasphemies. They no longer reached her, and she was certain they had not reached Jonas Hakluyt. Jonas was too far on the path of his own divine incarnation to take in Edward's aspersions.

"You have been and are my life, Edward," Mrs. Sawbridge spoke like one in a trance, "yet every breath I draw where you are concerned is sheer torture and anguish.... But he was no such thing, you fool. He was not!"

"Who, pet of my life, who are you speaking of now!"

She snivelled and choked, but managed to get out: "The Good Shepherd of course."

"And by the Good Shepherd you mean Jonas, sweetheart?"

"I mean the Savior, you infidel, Jesus Christ."

"But they are the same, don't you see? Jesus the Christ and Jonas Hakluyt.... Haven't you listened to your lover, Jared Wakeman, talk about Nietzsche and the Eternal Return.... Jonas was the Christ."

"Ah well, if you say so, Edward. You are always right." Her weary mind, her tormented nerves brought her back to the present. Jonas Hakluyt, like the Jesus of the stained glass

141

windows looking down on her taking communion was everywhere and nowhere. Her only thought now was she was facing eviction. Her earthly savior was leaving her. She looked over at him. He was applying some new hair-dye to his sideburns and mustaches with a tiny brush.

"I told you," he returned now to the soulless present, "I am not leaving you unprovided for. Of course, you must vacate your present quarters. But Mr. Niemoyer, I believe, has something even grander in mind for you."

"I knew he was!" Peg's mind wandered from all the months of insomnia. "But of course I knew Jonas was the Good Shepherd, all the while. What do you take me for?"

Jonas had been gone from them only two or three days, but it seemed a year, a lifetime. Desmond Cantrell and Jared Wakeman did nothing but quarrel. They were only dimly aware that Peg Sawbridge was being evicted from her tier of rooms. Worn out by their latest quarrel, Des fell asleep in Jared's arms.

Caressing him as he slumbered, Jared thought his dearest friend did not look right. He may have been cured of the Pest, Jared supposed, but he had through healing lost something very positive and bright. Yet there he was now, the only being he had ever truly loved, and he lay down at Desmond's feet and held tight to his legs, and moaned at the thought of winter coming.

As Des lay in this almost painful embrace, an envelope fell out from his shirt pocket to the floor beside Jared. The envelope was unopened. Jared had the gift of always recognizing bad news, even before he read a letter that contained it. He knew the letter inside would be very serious and even cataclysmic, but he was not fully prepared for the document the thick envelope contained. Jared had to read it several times to get the full significance of it all, the legal language and the stilted, phrases, the lawyer jargon drained of real human communication, a phraseology that made its real meaning more deadly.

"I see you opened it then, Jared," Des opened his eyes and gave his childlike, radiant smile. "Oh, I know what it says," he went on, "so you don't even need to read it to me. My Dad has disinherited me, I know, and allocated all his estate to my other two straight brothers. Dad found out about you and me, or I guess I should say, found out about me. My dad thinks all gays should be gassed – you know that."

Des waited. Jared held the letter with paralyzed hands.

Troubled, Desmond queried, "It don't make any difference, does it, Jared, that I'm poor now. When you said a while back that we'd be out on our ass when Peg is forced to give up her mansion here, I guess you didn't realize how true you spoke about us, did you! Jared, what is it? What's wrong with you?"

Desmond rose up, and his face paled almost as markedly as when he had been so ill.

"Of course it don't make any difference, Des," Jared spoke with bitter hurt. "The meanness of your Dad, though, knocks me over. I thought disowning went out with the horse and buggy."

"That's about where my Dad is. All he ever cared about was his horses and livestock. He told one of his business associates once within earshot of me that if one of his sons was ever found out to be queer he knew the courts would approve of his action."

Jared strode toward the door.

"Where are you going to now, for cripes sake?" Des all but screamed.

"I'll be right back, Des, baby. But I got to catch my breath."

"Catch it here, Jared.... Don't go now when you've just found out how much I need you. Don't go!"

But Jared had opened the door and bang-slammed it behind him.

Outside, he was sniffling and trying to prevent outright sobbing. Then, he heard the voices of Mrs. Sawbridge, Mr. Hennings, and the new voice of the wizard from the Street, Mr. Niemoyer.

One of Jared's incurable habits was eavesdropping, and he felt eavesdropping now was just the ticket for what he needed. The voices of Peg and Edward and the third voice reached him even through the thick panelling of the door he leaned on. The third voice, that of the Prussian, Ezra Niemoyer, dominated.

"Why should you fuss so, I ask you, my dear Edward," the voice thundered, though all Jared was really hearing was Des telling him again and again he was disinherited.

"I say, Edward, why do you care? You know I will provide for our lady here. She shall have better quarters than you have been bestowing her with. Of course I'll put it on paper. I have an elegant hostelry picked out for her. Fifty rooms, all to herself. But say I, Edward, what care you and I if the Great City is finished, that the half-breeds rule, that the Mayor is a hysterical night-club entertainer, flanked by crooks of every persuasion, that girls become mothers at ten, and babies are forced to wear condoms at birth, that no one works or can read or add, that the clitoris has replaced manhood as an idea. What, my dear friend, can it matter, if the Street and the Market flourish, if not here, abroad, and the Street will continue to flourish and be the by-all and be-all. Look at you! You've survived fifty disasters in your lifetime, and by Christ, you'll live to be as old as I. You are a youth. As to the hotel-hospital you've been running here for Madame Sawbridge"(here he probably, Jared felt, bowed to Peg, if his 100-year-old back would permit him) "and her staff, it must be closed. Weep not, Madame, weep not. You're provided for in a style after my fashion. I am a scale above our dear Edward, after all, in wherewithal and taste. I say, Edward, it's all right if young Evangelists are burned to a crisp and Thespians catch, die, or are cured of the Pest. But present company aside, dear Hennings, don't you see we need the Pest to clean up the race. And it's mostly a half-breed disease anyhow. Nature is like the Street, my good friend, the finest and best will survive. We're sailing into a greater future, that's all."

Jared flung open the door. His appearance was so ghastly,

Peg later reported to all who would listen as she packed her bags for her new domicile, yes, Jared looked so frightful even Ezra Niemoyer stopped in the middle of his homily.

"You may come in, Wakeman," Edward Hennings spoke with uneven tone, and his palsied hand loosened on his tie clasp.

"Mr. Niemoyer, Mr. Wakeman."

Rage, fear, or terror, always made Jared bereft of speech. He almost broke the extended hand of 100-year-old Ezra Niemoyer, then flung it aside like a styrofoam bag.

"Mummy!" he finally got out. "I heard you behind the mortgaged panelling. I heard." He began to weep violently.

"His own son! His favorite son!" Jared turned to Peg. As in his greatest roles Jared moaned, and then fell headlong, face downward, on the recently polished and waxed hardwood floor. "Dis-in-herited."

"He blamed me, of course, for everything," Peg Sawbridge often would confide to her few remaining intimates after her own disinheritance and the fall of her house.

"And what a fall, my darlings, it was," she talked over cracked tea cups in her new surroundings overlooking the river. (It was grander than the old tier of flats and floor-throughs, but to her, it was bleak, shoddy and styleless.) "But after the scandal," Peg went on, "after the immolation of the Young Preacher and the police and the press and the inquest!" (Here Peg put on huge rose sunglasses, for any great grief caused her eyes to throb and be unable to stand light of any kind. Even a tiny candle smote her optic nerve like an arrow.) "But then who blamed me," she went on. "Who said I was behind Desmond's being disinherited, and Jonas Hakluyt's murder, and Edward Hennings washing his hands of everyone? Who but Lucifer himself, Jared Wakeman!"

Jared Wakeman was sure after he read and reread the letter of Desmond's disinheritance that the Pest was still in his

145

lover's veins. There are no cures, are there? He talked to himself now all the time.

"And then," he went on, in his sotto voce soliloquy, "when Peg was thrown out of her collection of mansions and lots, penthouses and suites, granted, she is in a practically imperial palace, courtesy of the neo-fascist Niemoyer, she feels and acts like a bag-lady!"

Jared shuddered.

But beyond Peg's exile and his lover's being disinherited, Jared, for a young man who prided himself of being unshaken by any shift of fate, fortune or the congeries of natural phenomena, his hearing again of that cry in the night made his blood run cold. He shook like every ague in medical history. And a voice, like that of a Chuck-Will's-Widow bird was as clear in his eardrum as when he had first heard it. The Evangelist! Just before he left him for good!

Jared saw it, heard it all over again. He glimpsed himself trying the door behind which the sounds were issuing.

"No, no, don't enter," the bird warned him.

Then the door was flung open from inside and Jonas Hakluyt, wearing only a tiny cheap crucifix about his discolored, sinewy throat, stood there gaping at Wakeman.

In response to that desperate glance, Jared had made a sound almost as eerie as the Chuck-Will's-Widow bird.

"Drink it all in, my shame. Go ahead, Jared. Shall I turn on the upper lights?"

Jonas' case was so much more advanced than Desmond's even at Des' worst, that Jared threw himself down on the bed where Jonas had been writhing.

"I knew you would know," Jonas said and lay alongside Jared. "I knew once you had seen me you would know."

"You'll stand beside me, Jared," again and again and forever, the Thespian was to hear the sentence. He knew then he loved Jonas Hakluyt even more than he loved Desmond Cantrell. But it was a different love. He knew then Christ existed.

Jared blubbered something and tried to withdraw his hand

before it was fractured by the pressure of love, but the hand was retained as if it had been severed. "Give me your mouth," Jonas Hakluyt said, and Jared surrendered his lips to him. "Thank you for love," he thought the Evangelist said before he went out to die before his followers. "Thank you for the last kiss." It was Jared who also recalled in fine detail the rest of the epochal happenings the day the cicadas had quit their song, and the street was full of dry yellow sycamore leaves.

Mr. Hennings of course – who else, Jared reminisced, appeared at the top of the stairs. He did not so much look old as a something out of history itself. He appeared taller, though he was always tall of course, six feet three in his socks, and he carried a large black hatbox of some kind. He raised the box all at once above his head as if as a Bolshevik he had finally got hold of a bomb at last.

"Must you leave, Edward?" Peg's voice soared from the stairway of the floor above them. 'Just because those damned veined insects are no longer droning to their mates in the buttonwood trees in the square! And where are you going at your age? Be reasonable."

Mr. Hennings put down the box and looked upwards. They were perfect, Jared saw, for one of his plays. They were the soul of all drama.

"My only darling and my dearest dear," Mr. Hennings told her, just as if Jared had shoved the script in his gnarled hands. "Haven't I told you a thousand times you are provided for. Bag-lady, derelict! What matters if you loathe Mr. Niemoyer. You'll never see him where you're going. The fifty-room domicile is all yours. Besides, he may be lying in the morgue at this very moment in view of he's over 110. Remember too the little red boxes in the medicine cabinet when you feel your heart is fluttering. It always fluttered though even when you were a mere child. I'll send more of the little red pills."

"From where, darling, from where?"

"From there," Edward laughed. "Santiago. Santiago de Cuba."

Estrellita appeared from nowhere at the naming of their

147

destination, and clasped Edward's hand in hers. Her cheeks appeared brick-red over her copper complexion.

"Say goodbye to Desmond," Edward Hennings cried, as two chauffeurs appeared on the floor below and called his name. "Goodbyes are too suffocating, my angel." He kissed Peg Sawbridge.

"Edward, I will not survive this leave-taking," Peg whispered.

"Your left earring is loose, sweetheart," he pointed out. "Perhaps your lobe on that side needs piercing again. The pierced holes grow fast, you know, if not watched. My grandmother pierced her own of course."

"My lobes are perfectly open, my darling," Peg assured him and adjusted the emerald earring he had bestowed on her nearly a half century before. "I wish I had died in that terrible Chicago blizzard, Edward, of so long ago. I was so happy then, Edward, so blissfully, joyously happy.

"The Wrigley building you pointed out looked always like a giant nabisco, remember," she went on and on. "And the way we would wait for the Michigan avenue bridge to rise and then descend." Then, having wiped away her tears, she saw through her filmy pupils her Savior and Redeemer and with him, his wife-husband spouse were going, were gone. She heard the snort of the car engine and the scream of the tires.

"Death itself," she turned to Jared, "they say is just a little air passing through one's lips and nose."

In their private plane, Edward Hennings watched his wife not so much with worried concern as with deep curiosity. The thing about being so old is that one is gratified and rewarded in taking in every detail about everything around one.

"I can see, *querida*, that you have fallen under the spell of the Great Metropolis," Edward finally commented and kissed her hand devoutly.

"We left with the last cicadas," he laughed as he quoted Peg Sawbridge.

"You made everybody fall in love with you, Lita," he went on. "Everyone's heart went pitty-pat at the mere sight of you. But leaving so abruptly was your best ploy. Now they will love you forever because they will never see you or me again. I always do what is best for you. A little poison is health-conferring, but New York, the quintessential poison of our day, can only be taken in teeny teeny doses by outsiders. Those who remain over-long, die, inch by gasping inch, as the City itself is dying. Wasn't the pillar of salt really New York? It's always been poisonous and in bad taste, but of late, its bad taste and vulgarity and its bogus energy have become so all pervading that many visitors have to be hospitalized only a few days or hours after arriving at the Pillar.

"But ah, Estrellita, *amor mio*. How you deceived them all! Poor mad Peg, thinking you were a man, merely because you won't trim your pubic hair and so it hangs, priapus-like, down. And Jared loving you against the grain, thinking you were a girl and wondering therefore if he was a child of Sodom after all."

Jared Wakeman had the very bad habit of seldom opening his mail. Probably because most of the mail he received was unpaid bills. They had shut off his gas and light so many time, friends finally took over the courtesy of paying them for him. As to his landlord, that was an even more complicated affair.

But the foreign looking envelope made him even more procrastinatory. So it lay about for days, perhaps weeks. He would occasionally pick it up and stare at it, then put it down.

Then there was a call from a brace of attorneys on Wall Street. What they told him was, he thought, at first a joke on the part of some of his actors. In fact, he accused the different callers of being Thespians.

Finally, there was a severe call from an attorney whose name even Jared had heard of, a man close to the top of the canyons in Wall Street.

Then, with trembling hands, he opened the foreign, thick envelope, and read first the Spanish and then the translation.

They talk about Jared Wakeman being self-centered, so cruel, so egomaniacal, but at that moment he wondered only how he would breathe the news to Peg Sawbridge. He was afraid when he told her she would never want to act again, and he would be alone at last with Desmond Cantrell and his disinheritance.

"I'll go tell her," he said to himself. "I bet though, she dies in my arms."

One tiny tear broke out from his eyelashes.

Peg Sawbridge was surrounded by Thespians that cool October day in her new thimble-sized, matchbox apartment. Actually, it was even more splendid than her old salon, but true, it somehow, whether by reason of the autumn light or its not having been properly furnished, looked meaner and tinier than her old mansion.

She nodded to Jared who stood in the doorway holding the foreign envelope like a messenger boy from the past.

"Don't gawk, dear heart," she ordered him.

"I was just telling everyone," she flourished her hand to the assembled actors, "that beautiful as Estrellita's eyes were, they always reminded me of gooseberries."

Jared Wakeman sank down into one of the brand-new ottomans.

"After Ramon," Peg went on, oblivious to what was in store for her, "after that dearest of lads ran away to the Dominican Republic with a famous millionaire, I have been holding hands in sheer desperation with a pizza delivery boy."

Everyone applauded this intelligence.

"Dominick Gigli," she added, but no one in the room remembered the real Gigli, so the wit was lost on them.

"Like most New Yorkers, as Edward Hennings would say, Dominick, of course, cannot speak English, but I catch a word now and then of what I take to be Sicilian. What are words worth when there is good looks like his! As he serves me slice after slice of pizza, he allows me to also feast on the sinews of the crook of his arm where dark veins like little walnuts hide.

"I tell Dominick the story of my life as he and I munch contentedly the cheese and anchovy tidbits."

But gradually, Peg's words came out slower and slower like the time she had completely forgotten her part in a long play they were in together, Jared and she. "What is it?" she said, finally watching Jared. "For God's sake."

He brought the thick sheaf of papers out from the envelope.

"Peg of my heart, as Edward used to say to you," he began. "Now don't be jealous, sweetie, at my news." He waited, only because the phlegm in his throat was strangling him.

"Let me hear it!" she commanded, in just a shred of a voice.

"He has willed me, Peg, two theaters. I have been to Wall Street. I don't know who I am anymore, Peg. Did you hear, I have been to Wall Street."

Jared saw in relief then she knew the rest of his news, and the real news.

The actors gathered round her.

"When did it happen, Jared?"

He went over to her new davenport and sat down beside her. "I am a poor sort at opening mail, Peg, and even worse at breaking news."

"I knew Edward was gone the minute you opened the door," Peg said.

"He died over a month ago, and is buried in Santiago de Cuba, at his request."

How calm she was, how quiet, like the air before thunderstorms, and that was, Jared knew, a bad sign.

"There's more for you ahead, Peg," he said, and kissed her. She held his hand like a patient will grasp at the wrist of the anaesthetician.

"I wish Ramon was here," she managed to confide to him.

"A whole month he's been gone," she repeated.

He had always known that Edward Hennings was her love,

151

and her reason for existing at all, but when he saw how she was receiving his message he understood it at last. She allowed him then to kiss her hands as much as he cared to, except for a brief pause during which for some reason he did not understand, she took off her earrings and laid them in a little box behind her. Then she gave him her hands for him to kiss all he wanted.

"Just to think, though," she somehow was able to get out, "your dream of having your own theater, Jared. See, dreams do come true."

"*Theaters*, Peg. There are two of them."

But then, despite the fact his long-cherished dream had come true, the gift of the theaters without the presence of the giver seemed somehow hollow.